"Are you a psychic?" Sam asked

His laughter, as he said it, was forced.

"Only with you," she said.

"Alex? What is your real name?" He released her, becoming a black shadow an arm's length away, his voice strained. "Do you have some witch's vision that lets you look inside me?"

She reached out, her fingers touching the scar, feeling the rough crease it made on his face. "I feel as if I've known you forever. Does that bother you? I'm no danger to you. I don't even have a last name, nor do you. I'm just someone you dreamed up. I'll be gone when you wake."

"Some dream," he said roughly, catching her face between his hands, covering her lips with a fleeting, teasing caress. "I've never had a dream like you before."

VANESSA GRANT started writing her first romance at the age of twelve and hasn't forgotten the excitement of having a love story come to life on paper. After spending four years refitting the forty-six foot yacht they live on, she and her husband, Brian, and their teenage son set sail south to Mexico along the North American West Coast. Vanessa divides her time between her writing, sailing and exploring the harbors of the Pacific Coast. She often writes her love stories on her portable computer while anchored in remote inlets. Vanessa says, "I believe in love and in happy endings."

Books by Vanessa Grant

HARLEQUIN PRESENTS

HARLEQUIN ROMANCE

VANESSA GRANT

one secret too many

Harlequin Books

TORONTO • NEW YORK • LONDON
AMSTERDAM • PARIS • SYDNEY • HAMBURG
STOCKHOLM • ATHENS • TOKYO • MILAN

For Angela Marie

Harlequin Presents first edition August 1991
ISBN 0-373-11386-2

Original hardcover edition published in 1990
by Mills & Boon Limited

ONE SECRET TOO MANY

CHAPTER ONE

SHE was alone, looking out over glassy black water, streaks of coloured light stretching from tall buildings on the shore of English Bay.

In the darkness, her brown shoulder-length hair could have been black; but as she moved there was no mistaking the soft fineness of it caressing her shoulders. She was a little taller than average, walking the sandy beach slowly, feeling a seductive fullness in the silence. It was strange to her, this solitude. No one in the world knew where she was. No one would miss her if she stayed on the beach all night.

When the man appeared at the top of the hill, she felt no sense of intrusion. He walked the other way, claiming his own section of the waterfront, away from hers. She remained the only occupant of her world. At home she had her work cut out to steal a few solitary moments from each day, to slip up into her bedroom and write her stories in secret. Yet here in the city, this weekend, she had two whole days all to herself.

With the exception of today's frighteningly brief meeting with the agent, she might as well have journeyed the five hundred miles to spend her time alone. She pushed away memories of the meeting and her crazy, disastrous decision, and concentrated on the lights of the city.

What about the man? What made him pause at the water's edge and stare out? Somewhere near by an ambulance screamed. The man jerked as if the sound had penetrated to his core. He seemed to belong here in the eerie darkness, standing between the ocean and the buildings that held a million people. What did he think as he looked over her way? Did he see her at all?

Her mother would have apoplexy if she could see Mary out alone in the dark, standing on a lonely beach in the midst of the wicked city. But her mother would never know, would always believe that Mary had spent the weekend with a girlfriend. Mary was practised at keeping secrets. She had done it all her life, in self-defence. The secrets were getting bigger now, harder to keep.

The lights beckoned, whispering that the city was filled with people who took chances every day, who lived lives of adventure and change. 'Not me,' she whispered, 'but I bet he does.' There wasn't much you could tell from the distant form of the man against the sky, so it had to be her fancy, the overactive imagination that had made life difficult from her youngest days.

A sailboat at anchor rose up against the night sky, tall masts reaching into the unknown. It might have been a pirate ship ready to raise sail and slip away.

There he was, standing with legs astride, a silhouette against the sky. For a long, still moment they stared at each other. Then he moved, and she felt a sick, hysterical conviction that he was all the things she had been warned about. A madman. A pervert. Danger in the night, swooping down on innocent girls. Heaven knew she was innocent.

She should run, get to the lights and the people. A strange man. A lonely beach. He walked like a strong man. He would have hard, bulging muscles. He was a man who might walk out of the bush, or a wild man who would be at home living in the sparse, cold tundra.

Coward! She was afraid of bears, afraid of strange men. Afraid of life. Was there a magnet bringing him closer, holding him silent? What held her so still? Why this crazy, excited feeling that she was on the edge of a delicious adventure? Tomorrow she might be a cold statistic, a corpse discovered by early morning strollers.

He moved steadily until he was only a hand's reach away. She could see the deep, hard lines of his face in the moonlight. Unruly dark hair with a will of its own. He hooked his thumbs into his belt and seemed to relax, to wait for her to talk first.

'Where did you get the scar?' Was that her voice?

He touched the jagged mark high up on his left cheekbone. 'An accident in the bush.' His voice was deep and low, reassuring. 'I got in the way of a falling tree.'

'I thought maybe it was a street fight.' Her dark hair swung against her throat as she watched him touch the scar again, fleetingly. What would those fingers feel like against the soft, heated flush of her cheek?

He said, 'I hate to disillusion you, but I looked a bit like a gangster before the tree fell on me.'

A dangerous man. Even the street gangs would walk warily around him. She must be moonstruck, talking to him on a Vancouver beach. Alone. Anyone from the parish would be more than happy to tell her that she was on the sure path to ruin. She pushed her hair back with one hand, saw his eyes following her motion, giving it a sensuous significance.

He smiled and his face changed, the deep serious lines shifting to warmth and humour. 'Who are you? A spirit of the sands?' His hand reached towards her hair, but did not touch it. She drew back, yet, oddly, she was not afraid. His voice was easy, not threatening. 'It's not every night that I find a woman on the beach—and never one like you, with big brown eyes a man could drown in.'

It was too dark to see the colour of his eyes, but she couldn't seem to stop staring at him, watching him, wondering...

He said softly, 'I know. You're a beautiful wench escaped from the wicked captain of a pirate ship——' His voice faded abruptly and she had the strangest feeling that a faint flush was beginning to flow over his face.

'That's it,' she agreed quickly, bathed in the playful fantasy he had created. 'See? Out there? That's the ship of the villainous pirate. He stole me from the village where I was a young virgin, carrying me off into the night, away from my family.' *Virgin*. The word seemed to echo over the sands. She stepped back again, farther, her hands spread nervously as a barrier.

He murmured, 'Hard to blame him,' but his voice told her there was no threat here.

'I've escaped only this night. I swam through the cold waters.' Magic. Fantasy magic. She had never shared a fantasy before. 'I fought the treacherous current to reach this shore.' She waved away the houses on streets behind them, caused to vanish all the lights, concrete and asphalt. 'I seek sanctuary!' she declared dramatically.

She warmed to the smile that had started to play around his firm lips. 'Do you have a name?' She was amazed at the unwilling fascination in his voice.

'My name?' No one would believe that this was Mary Houseman. Tonight she must be another woman—something like *The Three Faces of Eve*. 'Call me Alex.' A girl named Alex wouldn't be bothered by talking to a strange man on a lonely beach.

Lights from a car on a nearby road crawled across the sand towards them. He shifted slightly to shelter her. 'I'm Sam——'

'No! I— Just Alex and Sam. That way we'll both be free to be...' The sailing ship was moving, slipping away through the darkness. Just a few minutes of crazy fun, a half-hour of harmless madness. She whispered, 'Shadows passing in the night.'

His whisper joined hers. 'All night would be nice.'

For a moment she almost wished she were the kind of woman who could take him up on that invitation. Until now she had never understood how a woman could meet a strange man and, in the space of a few moments or hours, be willing to walk with him into a dark room with a bed. She said desperately, 'I don't really belong here, and I'm just—I think I'm kind of crazy this weekend. Not really myself.' He didn't say anything. She said, 'I've never talked to a strange man in my life before.'

'Am I that strange?'

What was it about him? 'What colour are your eyes?' It must be Alex asking the question. For a moment she thought he was going to touch her lips with gentle callused fingers. Alex was a creature of fiction. For a non-existent lady, she was certainly getting out of hand. She gulped. 'I—I should go back.'

'Don't.'

That was all. Just one word. She bit her lip. 'I—I think you're a bit out of my league.'

A smile covered her glimpse of something dark in his face and he offered his hand to her. 'Then we'll play in your league, shall we?' She could feel the hard callus of his hand rough against her soft flesh. He was walking and somehow she was keeping pace, but stumbling in the sand, her bare feet reminding her that she had slipped her tights into her bag earlier. She gasped, 'Too fast! I'm in bare feet! Let me put my shoes on.'

He stopped and she got her hand back, bent over her shoes as he asked, 'What do you want to do? Something magic? Fantastic?' Somewhere there must be a wind blowing. The air was still around them, but the water had begun to surge in along the sand in slow whispers. 'Come on,' he urged gently. 'Tell me.'

She had never realised that there was such a collection of wild young desires boiling up inside her, never known she could be uninhibited enough to say to a stranger, 'I want all the things that are crazy and—I want to go to the zoo in the middle of the night and—I'm hungry. I'd like to eat something delicious and exotic in some insane place—the beach or the park. And go dancing somewhere my family wouldn't approve of. Laugh out loud even if people are staring, and dance fast and wild. Go for a walk across the bridge at three in the morning.'

'You really are running away.'

She was breathless, her heart pumping blood wildly through her veins. 'I'm supposed to be here for a weekend, visiting a college friend, having long lunches and going to the theatre.'

'Maybe even a trip to the museum?' he suggested. 'I have a feeling that your college friend might be the museum type.'

'Don't you think museums are interesting?' She wondered what he thought about anything. What did he think about her?

'They have their place, but not for a sea waif who's running away. We'll see what we can do about your list.' He made her desires seem reasonable. 'First the food, I think. Don't you?' She followed his lead, let his fingers hold hers, her shoes slipping in the sand.

She found herself asking, 'Sam, what are you running away from?'

'What makes you think I'm running?'

Instinct. She thought she was right. She could see him quite well in the lights from the street now. She didn't know where they were going, but men didn't come any tougher or harder than this one. She had no right to be walking with him, hands tangled together as if she was willing to let the night take its course.

He said, 'I don't do a lot of running. And you're breaking our rules. Sam and Alex. Anonymous strangers.' He stopped at a car, low and white and powerful. She wouldn't have been surprised right then if he had broken into it and hot-wired it, but he had keys and he held the door for her. 'Up to you,' he said wryly, leaving her by the open door, walking around and letting himself into the driver's seat.

Mary would have run.

Alex sank down on the cool leather upholstery and closed the door. He started the engine. It was muted and powerful. She looked out of the window. On the pavement a couple passed by arm in arm, laughing. Beside her, Sam seemed suddenly a hard man, dangerous. He said, 'You're quite right. I'm not the kind of man your mother would approve of.'

'What do you know about my mother?'

'Just a feeling.' She touched the leather upholstery and he grinned. 'The place I live in matches the jeans, not the car.' Then his voice was deep and sombre. 'I won't cause you any harm, Alex.'

She laughed then, joy surging up and overcoming her. 'Oh, I wish Emily Derringer could see this! She'd be so shocked! Seeing me getting picked up by a——' A wild man, dangerous, sexy. She blinked away Emily, found her fingers curling into Sam's when he reached across to take her hand.

He took her to an Italian restaurant where it didn't matter that his jeans were patched while her suit was silky and elegant. The air around them seemed to ring with soft, happy laughter. She knew she couldn't stop smiling. Maybe she looked silly, sitting there with a big grin on her face, but he wasn't laughing at her, and this had to be the most wonderful evening of pure escapist fun she had ever had.

'What now?' he asked when the dinner was done.

'Everything,' she said simply. She held out her empty glass and he poured another measure of the light, bubbly wine into it. Her heart thundered at the look in his eyes and she said quickly, 'Dancing. Music. Walking along the beach... Magic. I don't know, Sam. You choose.' Her heart wouldn't stop crashing against her ribcage. He might take any sort of invitation from those words.

He had a glass of beer in one hand. He liked beer more than wine, a curious detail of information about a man with no last name. His free hand reached across to touch the softness of her cheek lightly. Then he had her hand, was leading her to a small half-lit dance floor where the quiet music flowed over them. As his arms settled around her, his hands on her back, she wondered what it would feel like to have his hands touch the parts of her body that no one touched. To have his eyes see, his hard maleness possess...

Oh, lord! He could see every detail of what she was thinking. His arms tightened as she moved back from him. Her hands were pressed against his upper chest, feeling the hardness all through him as he drew her closer. This was crazy, insane! Dangerous!

She should get out of here. Get a taxi and get back to her hotel. Go into that room and lock the door and shiver and hug her body and try to remember that it was a mercy she had escaped——

'What's wrong?' His voice broke harshly through her wild thoughts. She was stiff in his arms, jerking instead of moving to the music.

Nothing could happen here. There were other couples—not many, but enough. There was the waiter leaning against a doorway, watching them dance, looking a little bored with a slow evening. Her arms slipped up around his shoulders, his neck, and he didn't ask her again what was the matter. He just brought her closer with hard, warm hands.

She should remember this feeling. She could use this in her next book, the lazy warmth that was surging through her. The way her breasts were swelling. The way every part of her seemed to be crying out to be closer, to touch, to feel. In a book, her heroine could be rash and reckless, could let the desires take control and——

He was watching, seeing the images flood wildly across her mind, the hot flush of abandon coursing through her body. She licked dry lips, a nervous gesture that transformed itself into a sensuous invitation as his eyes watched.

She turned her head, let her face bury in the hard security of his shoulder. His voice was very low, husky with desire. 'I don't think I'm ever likely to forget tonight.' Then his arms tightened, his fingers digging into the flesh of her back, telling her without words what it was that he wanted. He was strong, a tough man who would win any battles he chose to fight. In his eyes were the scars of battles he didn't talk about.

Her fingers reached up to touch his cheek. 'Tell me about the tree that fell.' She frowned, said, 'Do you mind my asking?'

She liked the way his grin was a little lopsided. 'I don't mind telling you.' He turned to avoid another couple, drew her back against his broad chest. 'I was working as a faller on the Queen Charlotte Islands. Logging. About ten years ago. Ancient history for you.'

'I'm not that young.'

'Aren't you?' How old was he? Thirty-five? Forty? He said wryly, 'I don't suppose I was as good a logger as I might have been. Not careful enough, anyway.'

He described the ancient forests of the southern Queen Charlottes, the scattering of Haida Indians who had been demonstrating against logging on the island. 'One of the Haidas—Jake—was an artist from Vancouver on holidays, visiting his mother's family and embroiled in the local politics. He and I had been enjoying arguing off and on for about three days, each of us on opposite sides of the native picket-lines.' She felt him shrug, found herself relaxing closer against his chest. 'It was a pretty informal protest. The chief and the head of the logging operation were on first-name terms, and quite a few of the fallers were Haidas, too. Jake spent a lot of time sketching.'

She couldn't see his face, but his voice sounded very casual, as if he were describing something he had read in the newspaper. 'I must have made the cut wrong. When the tree started to go, I realised that I wasn't clear at all. I couldn't see where Jake and the other fellow were. I remember shouting to them, then I ran, but— not fast enough or far enough.'

She could feel the tension in his muscles, then he shrugged it away and his hands gentled against her back. 'I don't remember the rest. Jake apparently got a tourniquet on my leg. I guess it was bleeding pretty bad. When I woke up, I was in hospital in Vancouver.' His hands moved restlessly over the silk of her dress.

'That's the story,' he said, and she had the feeling that it was only the beginning, but knew he was not going to tell the rest.

Then there were no more words, only the music and the dancing, the man and the wild stirrings that were Alex and not Mary. Time flowed into the night, and she had lost the moments, the hours, when he whispered against her hair, 'Let's get out of here. Let's go somewhere we can be alone.'

She looked up at him, her eyes wide and nervous. He said softly, 'It's all right. I'll look after you. I'll protect you.'

She thought she might follow anywhere if he was leading the way. She watched in a delightful haze as he paid the bill, then she took his hand and followed him out to the street. She was hugging her light suit jacket against herself and feeling a cold breeze coming off the shadowed buildings. A man and a woman walked past them, both swaying as they walked, laughing at some secret joke, and Mary could see herself, following where Sam led with his hand gripping hers, and she knew exactly what Emily Derringer would have to say about all of it.

Sam unlocked the door of his car and Mary panicked, looking at the open door, at Sam's face with the dark, intense shadows. 'No, let's—I want to walk.'

'Here?' He was smiling at her, laughing a little, and that made it easier to meet his eyes, then to look around and see that it wasn't the kind of area where you should walk if you wanted to avoid being mugged—or worse.

'Somewhere else? Somewhere there's grass and trees?'

He shrugged, and she saw the moment when the tension left him, when he decided that he was not going to take her to whatever dark place it was that he had planned for her seduction.

He took her to Lost Lagoon. It was quiet with the lights reflecting on water, a twisting path for their feet to follow as they moved away from buildings, alongside the trees. There were sounds of wildlife, but they were gentle sounds. Birds, she supposed, although everything should be asleep by this hour.

Tonight was totally out of character, and never to be repeated again. She knew why she was here. For the first time in her life she had the opportunity to be anonymous, to be impulsive and crazy. For one short weekend it was irresistible. Also, perhaps she was hiding from the repercussions of that meeting with the agent today. The contract signed. The book, impossibly, going to press.

It was so dark now that there was no way that she could see even the form of his face when she looked at him. But his hand had slipped from hers and he was walking with sureness in the dark, his arm around her waist, her body leaning against his just a little. She found herself asking again, 'What are you running away from tonight?'

'Other people's tragedies.' Although he spoke lightly, she thought his words were serious.

Her father spent much of his life with other people's pains, but this man was no healer of souls. Too many of his emotions were held tightly inside, although she thought it would be good to have him close if you needed raw strength of spirit.

'Somebody died?' She knew it was true.

'Are you a psychic?' His laughter was forced.

'Only with you,' she said.

'Alex? What is your real name?' He released her, became a black shadow an arm's length away, his voice strained. 'Do you have some witch's vision that lets you look inside me?'

She reached out, felt her fingers touching the scar, feeling the rough crease it made on his face. 'I feel as if I've known you forever. Does that bother you?' She saw that it did. 'I'm no danger to you. I don't even have a last name, nor do you. I'm just someone you dreamed, and I'll be gone when you wake up.'

'Some dream,' he said roughly, catching her face between his hands, covering her lips with a half-angry kiss that suddenly gentled into a fleeting, teasing caress. 'I've never had a dream like you before.'

Then he wasn't touching her at all. Her hand dropped away from him and she was standing filled with a nervous excitement, her lips tingling and parted as if waiting for his kiss again.

He turned away. She found herself following, her feet somehow sure on the black path. She swallowed, closed her lips, tried to feel as if a man's hard kiss meant nothing. She pictured him in the living-room of the house she lived in, with her father in his cleric's collar and her mother's sharp eyes watching. He didn't fit, would never fit.

But tonight she was Alex, and Alex could never fit into Mary's place. She said softly, 'Will it make it easier if I tell you my secret? You can laugh, and I won't mind.'

He was still, held by her voice, and she told him, 'Alex is my fantasy name. I wrote a book and used Alex Diamond for a pen-name. I never thought it would sell. But—I came down to Vancouver, from the North Coast, to tell my agent that it's impossible, that I can't sell the book after all.' She shook her head, the hair flying around, and said wildly, 'But somehow I signed the damned thing, the contract. I shouldn't have, but I did.'

'Why not sell it?'

She said wryly, 'The book's not exactly the sort of thing a minister's daughter should write. I called it *Holy Murder*, and it's totally fictitious, although I have to admit that the villain does resemble Mr Warbothle, not that I meant him to, but—and it's a love story, too. When I wrote it I never really expected to see it in print, so I let my imagination go. And if it ever got into print, someone would realise that it was me.'

'Why?'

'Because the murder took place in church—in the Sunday school, actually, during the service. And—oh, just everything! It's impossible! Everyone will read it, just to see what it said. Then they'd start wondering, aloud, whether I was writing about myself—how else could I——? Well, then my father would be upset by the talk, and my mother would be angry.'

'And Emily Derringer?' he suggested. She was amazed that he remembered about Emily.

'Oh, yes, Emily would get in on the act. She'd read it first, terribly shocked, and lend it to everyone else with the steamy passages marked.'

He grinned. 'Sounds like a book worth reading.'

She pushed at her hair with both hands, a frantic gesture that revealed more than she knew yet failed to tame the soft cloud of her hair. 'I could never stay at home if that book came out and people found out.'

'Then leave home. Move out.'

'You make that sound so easy, as if——' He talked like a man who had no home, who could never understand her hesitation. 'Let's forget it. Let's talk about ships or—anything else.' She bit her lip, said, 'You must think I'm a coward, afraid of what people——'

He was staring at her. She felt abruptly conscious of her own body. She shook her hair back and he said raggedly, 'I'd better take you back to——'

'No, not yet.' She would never see him again, never know the touch of his lips on her flesh, his body against hers. 'Dance with me again. Just once.' He was still silent and she said, 'I know there's no music, but——' She went into his arms, closing her eyes and hearing the music that wasn't there.

He had called her the pirate's wench. Sam's wench, she thought, moving so that her curves fitted more closely against him. She tipped her head back, looking up at him, their feet moving on soft grass. They glided away from the light, deep into a secret darkness where the trees sheltered the world from them. Her lips parted and his head bent, touching her mouth with a soft promise.

'Alex... Alexandra... You should have a knight on a white charger.'

'Knights are very overrated,' she murmured, her lips burning as they brushed against his. He had said he would protect her, and despite her innocence she knew what he meant. A good thing, she thought wildly, because things were slipping away, Mary was slipping away, and Alex was a reckless wench.

CHAPTER TWO

IF ANYONE was responsible for Sam's decision to turn down a posting as surgeon at the hospital, it was probably Jake. His friend turned up in emergency one night, frowning and abstracted as if he were in the midst of some artistic inspiration.

Sam's whites were rumpled from a busy shift, his chin showing the shadow of his beard. Technically, it was his day off, but as usual he was filling in for one of the residents. He gave Jake a comprehensive look. 'Social call? Broken leg?'

'Nope. My Indian blood keeps me healthy.'

Sam scrawled something incomprehensible on a form. 'How's Jenny? And the baby?' He was glad to see Jake, but typically he concealed his pleasure.

'They're fine. Jenny wants to know when you're coming to dinner. We haven't seen you in over a month.'

'Sorry.' The form went on to a pile of similarly incomprehensible papers and he started filling out another. 'I've been pretty busy.'

'This isn't your territory, is it? Aren't you surgery these days? How many hours a week are you putting in?' Sam shrugged the questions off and Jake persisted, 'Anywhere around here we can talk?'

In the little staff kitchen Jake refused coffee. 'I think you mix disinfectant with the water. You look terrible, Sam. Quade's worried about you, too. He says you're driving yourself harder than ever.'

Sam frowned, knowing he would not put up with this from anyone else. Jake had to stop talking when a patient

22

came into emergency with a cut hand. Stitches and
calming words, a couple of pain-killing pills. Jake was
still waiting afterwards and Sam sighed, asking, 'Is this
really your business?'

'Yes. If you had a wife or a girl it would be her
business. Since you're so damned determined to keep
everyone out of your life, it's got to be me. Don't you
think it's time you grew up and left the shelter of this
great institution? If you don't want to specialise, Quade
says it's time you got out into general practice.'

Sam rubbed at the scar where a muscle wanted to
twitch when he was tired. 'Damn it, Jake! I might have
been overworking a bit, but—Quade's short-sighted
about this. Nothing will satisfy him but seeing me move
out into general practice. He's got this notion——'

Jake could see someone coming through the emergency doors and knew that Sam would be busy again in
a minute. Jake's voice turned harsh. 'I think it's more
than overwork. I think you're afraid to go out into the
real world. You've been hiding for years—going to sea,
going up into the bush, university dorms, hospitals.
You've gone anywhere you could to avoid any hint of
family life.'

If the hospital had become a hiding-place for him, it was
a comfortable refuge, one he liked. But Jake's words
kept echoing in Sam's mind, reinforced by his own
knowledge that he was drinking too much coffee, getting
too little sleep. If he kept it up, he'd have high blood-
pressure and an ulcer himself. For the first time in his
adult life, Sam found himself thinking about buying a
house, getting furniture, making a home.

Alone, of course. He had no intention of sharing his
life with anybody, although perhaps he would get a dog.
He grinned at a vision of himself as an ageing general

practitioner with his pipe and his dog, a fireplace and a hearthrug. An old man who sometimes dreamed about the girl with silky brown hair, her cool, pale flesh burning under his kisses.

Her memory had the elusive magic of a dream, although it wasn't the kind of dreaming that Sam was accustomed to. He had spent more than one night dreaming his way through intricate surgery. He could not remember ever dreaming before about a woman who smiled and tipped her head back so that her hair flowed softly over her shoulders; waking with his heart thundering hard and wild in his breast—not with the terror of childhood nightmares, but with the joy of anticipation.

Sometimes there had been a woman in his life, although never anyone who mattered. In the last few years, the risks of casual affairs had become high enough that Sam had become almost celibate. He put his energy into the hospital.

Alex. But that was not really her name. One crazy night, and he would never see her again. He knew enough psychology to realise why she had such strong appeal, why she haunted his sleep. She was the perfect woman, alluring and sensuous, yet comfortably impossible. He didn't know her name, wouldn't know where to start looking for her. She didn't exist.

He confronted an odd fear in himself. If he left the hospital, went into private practice, the patients would be the same people week after week, year after year. He would get to know them, form relationships among them. In an impersonal way, it would be almost like developing a family.

Yet the idea of moving out of the hospital had been haunting him for weeks, ever since the day Quade had approached him, saying, 'I've got a GP from the North Coast in my office. I want you to talk to him.'

A general clinic, three doctors, and the practice growing so that they needed four now. They required a good surgeon, but one who didn't mind taking on a varied case-load. The clinic was too small to keep a surgeon busy full-time. Quade's recommendation of Sam's surgical ability had been important. Sam had talked to the GP, and had been tempted but wary. He'd stalled on his decision.

Later, Quade had taken him aside to insist that the variety would be good for him, and now Jake was getting on the bandwagon. He had to decide soon, but he had been uneasy from the beginning. He was used to the hospital, and hadn't the faintest idea how to go about setting up a home for himself outside.

And now, Alex. Alex was from up north, but surely it wasn't likely that she would turn up in this particular town. Lots of towns in the north.

Maybe it was Jake's visit that finally pushed Sam into saying yes. Or the vision of a fireplace of his own? More likely, a desire to prove to both Jake and Quade that he was not afraid to leave the hospital. That was a joke, a thirty-eight-year-old man trying to prove that he had no fears. Jake would laugh about that.

Alex wouldn't laugh. He had a rather frightening feeling that she would understand, and he was glad that their single night was an isolated, never-to-be-repeated event, a woman who would stay in his dreams, never again in his arms.

After years of hospital life, the change came suddenly and with frightening smoothness. There was really no one to say goodbye to, only Quade and Jake. Little to pack, just a few boxes sent up by courier. Himself, driving north on a two-day trip that moved his life from the familiar to the strange.

The North Coast. He'd always liked the tall evergreens, the frontier feeling of being away from the city. Crazy, because he'd been a city brat as a child, but those months out in the bushes of the Queen Charlottes had bred in him a love of the wild Canadian North.

In his new work, he found himself fitting into the clinic with little feeling of strangeness. The staff had the same brisk efficiency that he was used to in the hospital, although he found the personal questions disconcerting.

'Where are you from? Isn't that an American accent?'

'Is your wife coming up to join you?'

'Where are you staying...? Oh, looking for a house? Why, I know of——'

It took about half a day for everyone in the clinic to know that he was not bringing a wife or girlfriend up to live with him, was thinking of looking for a house to buy, and did not have any pets. He must be getting soft, or old. The Sam who had left Vancouver a few days ago would never have answered any of the personal questions.

His first Thursday had him dashing from the clinic to the hospital in response to an emergency call. A car accident, a bad one. At first he wasn't sure if he could save the life of the boy who had been in the passenger seat. At one point in the surgery, the anaesthetist said, 'That's it. He's going. I'm losing him.' But Sam refused to give up and, in the end, miraculously, the boy survived surgery.

The kid had injuries that took more than sewing. Sam spent most of the evening in intensive care, not able to do much except will the boy to fight his way through and live. Just before midnight he left to get some sleep.

He was afraid he would have to take the kid back into surgery, and he knew he needed rest first.

He was woken again at three in the morning. Once more to surgery, and again the kid somehow managed to hold on to his life. Afterwards, Sam dictated notes on the case into a microphone at the nursing station, blinking and seeing double and realising that he was sleepier than he had thought.

'Dr Dempsey?' It was the night nurse who had helped him in intensive care. 'Dr Dempsey? Would you mind talking to the other boy for a minute? The one who was driving? He's Dr Box's patient, but he wanted to see you.'

The boy's name was Neil MacKenzie. He had been lucky enough to get off with a broken arm and a cut head. He was seventeen, which meant that he was old enough to be tried as an adult, old enough to go to gaol for car theft. That could easily be keeping him awake.

'Pain?' asked Sam, looking down at the boy's pale face.

'Naw.' Neil MacKenzie winced as he shook his head, the blond curls lying trapped against his forehead by the bandage. 'I just wanted to know about Ripper.'

'Ripper?' Sam slipped his hands in his pockets, blinked, and tried not to look as if he was in a hurry to get back to his bed.

'My buddy. Is he bad? Is he gonna make it?'

'I'm hoping he will.' Sam folded his arms across his chest, watching the boy, the tiredness gone.

'If he dies, it's my fault.' The young voice trembled. 'The whole bloody thing was my idea. We had a bet that I couldn't get into that Chrysler and hot-wire it before the guy came back out of the pub.'

So Neil had won the bet, but he might have killed his friend. 'He might make it,' said Sam, his voice gentle under the roughness. 'If he can fight his way through the next twelve hours, I'm hoping he'll be out of danger.'

Neil MacKenzie. Not quite your ordinary trouble-maker. Sam took a look at his chart before he left the floor. No next of kin given. Someone had made a note that he was a ward of the court. Another street kid, thought Sam, feeling a crazy kind of kinship with the boy.

By the next evening Ripper was out of danger, so over the weekend Sam went house-hunting and discovered that he enjoyed poking through old houses. He couldn't remember ever doing anything like this before in his life. He looked at some of the modern, spacious homes on Graham Avenue, but it was the old pre-war homes that really appealed to him with their dormer attic-rooms and their sprawling inefficiency.

He had almost decided to make an offer for the two-storey wooden house overlooking the harbour. Lord knew what he would do with all that room, but he had his lips open to make an offer when he frightened himself with a mental picture of Alex drying her hair in front of the fireplace.

What the hell was he doing? Buying a house to give himself a background setting for the fantasies? He stalled the estate agent and tried to get Alex's images out of his mind, to think about the house alone. Property owner. That had a sound of permanency that was both tempting and frightening. The only thing of any substance that he owned was his car.

It looked as if Jake knew him better than he knew himself. He was terrified of relationships, families, dark-haired girls with eyes that looked right through his protective covering. He dreamed about her, the dream strong and real as it had been in the first few days after he had made love to her. He dreamed the feel of her;

the carefree, sweet pleasure of walking hand in hand with her at his side, listening and talking with her. Alex in his arms... Alex smiling, throwing the long hair back... Alex, shy and warm.

Then, finally, the sweetness ran its course and all the old memories surged up from where they should have been buried. The fights and the words of love followed by the violence and nights spent lying awake, shivering and waiting for mornings that never came.

She could feel the night air all around, warm and seductive. In the dream, her name was Alex...

She was walking beside the water, cool waves drifting in. Her sandals hung by their straps from the fingers of one hand as she watched the water, the erotic caress of sand and surf around her toes.

She felt him watching long seconds before she could turn. His eyes held her prisoner, then freed her to look at him. In the moonlight he was dark and dangerous. He moved just one step closer, and she could see the harsh planes of his face, the jagged scar high on his cheekbone. Behind him, city lights stretched across the still water.

Surrounded by a million people, yet they were alone. Alex. And the dark stranger. There was only blackness where his eyes should be, but they held, probing deep into her. As the tide surged higher, she was filled with warmth like a flame in the cold wastes of the Arctic.

She lifted her arms, reaching out to him. He receded as she came closer. She cried out his name...

'Mary!'

No, that was wrong. Her name was Alex...

His hands dragged across her flesh, receding, fading. She reached out, but he was gone and she was swimming—no, drowning in panic and some other

emotion. She pushed desperately at blankets twisted into
a prison around her, fighting her way to consciousness...

'Mary! Mary, get up!'

She managed to free the covers, and swung her bare
legs over the side of the bed, feet touching the cold
wooden floor.

'Mary! You——'

'I'm coming, Mom!' She stood up, pulling her
practical cotton nightgown up over her head and tossing
it on to the bed behind her. She stared at her vanity
mirror, seeing the brilliant blue sky, her own rumpled
figure. She pushed back the dark brown hair tangled
around her face.

The slender curves of her body looked smooth and
innocent. She didn't look like the kind of a girl who
would dream about a man like Sam, calling out with
need and yearning as if——

She brushed hard, transforming the tangle into a soft
brown curtain falling to her shoulders. Nice, Sam had
said, his voice oddly hoarse as he had touched her hair
with callused hands. She had wanted to melt into his
arms right then, just listening to the rough emotion in
his voice, seeing his harsh face, the soft, uncomfortable
vulnerability in his deep brown eyes.

'Mary!' The voice came from the foot of the stairs
below, demanding and imperative.

She attacked the hair again with her brush, as if stiff
bristles could erase the memories. 'Give me five minutes,
Mom! I'm just getting dressed!'

But she couldn't seem to move. The dream had hold
of her still, and the memories. 'Fantasy,' she said softly,
talking to the girl in the mirror. Brown eyes looked back
at her. Nothing special, she decided, meeting those eyes
with defiance. A brown girl. Eyes. Hair. Smoothly
tanned skin. Slender. A nice enough figure. Sam had

liked it. She touched herself hesitantly, almost unwillingly.

Hardly a girl by this time. She was twenty-five. A woman without a man. A woman who dreamed too much, spent too many nights alone with her fantasies. A woman whose mother was about to come up the stairs and forcibly drag her downstairs.

Not an innocent girl any more. One night. One night to remember forever, a secret to keep. 'Alex,' he had whispered, his hand pushing the soft hair back, his lips just a breath away from her mouth. 'You're magic...my mysterious, magic Alex.'

Alex Diamond. Fantasy lady. Her eyes sought and found the small computer on her desk, the collection of floppy disks that held her fantasies.

'Mary!'

She pulled open a drawer and rummaged for bra and panties. This was daytime, reality time. Time for Mary Houseman, not Alex Diamond. Alex was a lady of the night, and if Alex hadn't typed at the computer for long hours last night, while everyone else had been sleeping, she'd have let Mary get up in time to avoid her mother's demanding voice.

Downstairs her mother was moving about the kitchen with frightening efficiency. Mary poured herself a cup of coffee and braced herself for the onslaught.

'First,' said Frances Houseman briskly, 'your father had to go out early. The Connister funeral. Old Mrs Connister is upset, and he had to talk to her. She needs someone to go back home with her, to keep her company on the ferry.'

Mary stirred sugar into her cup, then picked up the jug of thick cream. 'When?' she asked, then, 'Who?' although she had a very good idea who would be volunteered to keep Mrs Connister company.

'I said you would do it.' Frances Houseman pushed the plug into the sink and squirted just the right amount of washing-up liquid in. 'After all, you've nothing important to do, have you?'

'No. Nothing much.' Just her new book, she thought sadly, but she could not tell her mother about that. She let a brief fantasy take hold for a moment. She would stand up, facing her mother and taking advantage of the fact that she was an inch or so taller. What would she say? 'Sorry, Mother. I can't. I've just got to get to work on this new book. My publisher's waiting.' Then she would walk away, upstairs into the room where the fantasies roamed free.

'Did you hear me, Mary?' Frances' hands were poised above the dish-water, bubbles of soap clinging to the fingers.

'Yes, Mother.' She took a sip of the coffee. 'You want me to accompany Mrs Connister back home on the ferry. When?'

'Next Wednesday. Have some cereal.'

'I'm not hungry.' She took another mouthful of the coffee. It sat uncomfortably on her stomach. 'Do you want me at the funeral?' She hadn't known Mr Connister, but her mother might feel it was appropriate for Mary to go.

'No. I'll be there, and your father's doing the service, of course. Just look after the phone, would you? And get across to the church. Your father left some letters for you, and I think the bank statement's come. He was saying that things are piling up a bit, so if you could just—oh, and Mary, I made an appointment with Dr Box for you—at three tomorrow afternoon.'

'I'm not sick.'

Frances attacked the table with a damp dishcloth, wiping away invisible specks of dirt. 'I'd like you to have a check-up. You haven't been right since you came back from Vancouver. I'm not sure you didn't pick up something down there.'

Mary choked on the coffee.

'A virus,' said her mother briskly. 'There's sure to be something going around, and Dr Box should have a look at you. Maybe you need a course of antibiotics.'

Normally it would be easier to waste a half-hour of the doctor's time, and her own, than to argue. Mary had learned years ago to let her mother have her way, to live her own life secretly, out of reach of busy interference. This time, though, she was uneasy about going to the doctor. For the last few weeks, a nervous fear had been growing inside her.

Surely it wasn't possible? Sometimes that incredibly passionate night seemed like a dream, but it had been real. So had the precautions been real. Sam had taken measures to protect her. She shuddered, remembering a friend of her mother's admitting that the last child had been an accident, that they'd taken precautions, but of course there was nothing that was a hundred per cent sure.

No! Of course it wasn't that. Just once in her whole life. One night, and she'd obeyed all the rules, or rather, Sam had. No, it would be just one of those things. Maybe she was late because of the emotional upset, or maybe it was just plain nature pulling tricks with her schedule.

Her father came in as Frances efficiently collected Mary's half-finished coffee and poured the warm liquid down the sink. Mary reached after the cup, then shrugged, meeting her father's warm eyes and laughing silently with him. Later, in the church office, she would make herself a cup of instant and sit quietly with it, taking her time.

'Hi, Dad. How's Mrs Connister holding up?'

'Not badly,' he said, bending to give her a morning kiss. 'Mary, I wonder if you——'

'I know. Next Wednesday. I'll go on the ferry with Mrs Connister. Mother told me.'

'Oh, good.' He stood, looking around with slight confusion in his eyes, as if he had forgotten why he was there. Then he remembered. 'Frances, I'll need a new shirt for the funeral. Mrs Connister's granddaughter spilled pabulum all over mine.'

Frances looked shocked and Mary giggled. 'Did they have you feeding the baby, Dad?'

He looked tall and thin and a little embarrassed. 'Well, things are a bit disorganised over there. Sometimes practical help is the best thing one can do. Mary, there's a letter from Lexie on the counter. Came this morning.'

She had found the envelope and was slipping the pages out as her mother came back with the clean shirt. 'She's with a man,' said Frances tightly.

Mary was reading quickly, even as she repeated automatically, 'Aunt Lexie? A man?' It was true. 'They're going sailing. In Alaska now, planning to head down for Mexico in— Hey, isn't that something! Good for Aunt Lexie!'

'She's living with him!' said Frances. 'A man with a ridiculous name. Not married or anything. She doesn't even mention marriage.'

Mary read the rest of the letter quickly. Her mother looked shocked. Even her father seemed uncomfortable at his sister's behaviour. Mary thought it was romantic. After all those years alone, her aunt had found someone—was starting out on a sailing adventure, for heaven's sake!

Wouldn't that be a plot for a book? Just look at the way they had met! Mary tried to imagine her eccentric aunt answering an advertisement in the personals and

ending up at sea with the man. No wonder her mother
was shocked, although Mary could well believe it was
something that Lexie might do. She giggled, then sobered
under her mother's stern eyes. 'I'll get over to the
church,' she said hurriedly.

Her father had made a mess of the correspondence
files in the church office. Mary sorted everything back
into its place, then tried to figure out which of the letters
needed answering. None of them seemed all that urgent,
so she made a few notes and left the correspondence in
order to attack the bank statement.

Later, she used the archaic church typewriter to knock
out her weekly article for the newspaper. She had been
down to the waterfront the day before, and she had
material for a whole series of articles. This week's was
the story of a sailboat from Tahiti that was cruising the
Pacific Rim in the tradtional manner—no radios, no
modern navigation aids at all. Personally, Mary thought
it was romantic, but crazy, and it made an interesting
column for the paper.

She got the article finished before the footsteps echoed
through the church, nervous voices carrying along the
corridor. She went out and found a couple with two
children. The man was about Mary's age, the woman a
couple of years younger. They had nowhere to sleep.

She showed them to the lounge where a big chester-
field folded out, and showed them the stove where they
could cook, because that was what her father would have
done. They had sleeping bags, and Mary had the telephone number of a sympathetic social worker.

'And of course you'll come to dinner tonight at the
parsonage,' she told the exhausted young mother. Lord,
the woman looked as if she was expecting yet another
child, and the two she already had were hardly out of
nappies. Didn't she know about birth control?

Nervously, Mary's hand went to her own abdomen. Was it fantasy, or was her skirt fitting a little more tightly?

She phoned her mother to tell her that dinner had to stretch to four more, but Frances must have gone out to the funeral parlour already, so Mary pedalled her bicycle back home and got a large roast out of the freezer, then left a note for her mother.

She took her motor scooter out, which would have caused her mother to raise her brows, but it was small and easy on fuel, and somehow Mary hadn't the extra energy today to pedal her bicycle. It had been Toby's scooter once, and she wasn't sure why she had resisted her parents' insistence on selling it after Toby's death. Perhaps it was a symbol of the independent spirit she had never had.

She stopped the scooter at the very top of the hill, letting the motor die to silence, and taking a moment to look out over the harbour. The sun was shining, but there were heavy clouds looming in the west. She hoped that wasn't symbolic of her own life.

There were three big ships in port, lying at anchor waiting to take on cargo. One was from Russia, the others might be from Japan or China. A couple of sails white against the blue water. On this side of the harbour, houses climbed up the hilly terrain. On the far side, beyond the water as far as she could see, untouched evergreen forest stretched to the north. She would have liked to stay, watching the water all afternoon—but tomorrow was the doctor.

What if her worst fears were true? Dr Box would know, and there would be a test ordered. Then it wouldn't just be Dr Box knowing, but the world. There would be a note on her file about the strange, groggy nausea she had in the mornings, the unaccustomed fullness of her breasts. Her file, and Dr Box's secretary was in the church choir. Emily Derringer was the town gossip, and Emily would find out somehow. Oh, lord! Emily's best friend was a lab technician up at the hospital. And ethics or no ethics, a possibly pregnant Mary Houseman was startling enough to ensure that the news would spread. Emily had always been nice to her in the past, but this would change everything!

They would all think the worst.

The parish would know. Then, somehow, inevitably, her parents would know. The thought of facing her mother was terrifying enough, but if her father thought she was the kind of girl who—— She shivered at the hurt she could imagine in his eyes.

Wild. Like her brother Toby, her Aunt Lexie.

Involuntarily, her fingers spread out across her abdomen. It was horrifyingly easy to believe that those hours with Sam could have borne fruit. Sam. It had been almost like a dream, a fantasy. She had come home from Vancouver, telling herself that that was what it had been. Not a crazy, wild and passionate storm that had swept over her life. Just a fantasy. Surely one fantasy would not get a girl pregnant?

If only she could be sure, and erase this horrible fear without the hospital lab. She bit her lip, wondering if there was a chemist in town without someone she knew at the cashier's counter. There were tests you could buy in the chemist. She had heard Bart Holley's girlfriend telling Bart that it was OK, she'd got the kit from the chemist and taken the test. Bart didn't have to worry.

Mary just hoped that it would be that way for her, that Mary wouldn't have to worry.

There were three chemists all within a couple of blocks of each other. Mary ended up at the closest, the chemist on the lower floor of the shopping mall. Surely if she bought one of those kits, it would prove that everything was OK. She simply could not be pregnant. It was impossible, wasn't really true. She saw the contraceptive devices for men there in the aisle, bit her lip and knew she didn't have the nerve to pick up a box and read what it said. Would it say something about reliability? She jerked her head around and no one was looking, but if she picked up that box, lord knew who would pop out of the woodwork.

'Can I help you?' She jumped guiltily, looking up at the man with the white jacket, the name-plate identifying him as the pharmacist. He was tall and friendly-looking. She couldn't remember his name, but he had been in her English class the year she graduated from high school. Now, it seemed, he was the pharmacist, and he recognised her at once. 'Hey, you're Mary, aren't you? Mary—ah——'

'Houseman,' she supplied. She tried to smile at him.

He looked around at the shelves filled with patent medicines. 'Looking for something? Can I help?'

She shook her head in energetic denial. 'Just killing time. Thanks, though. I didn't know you were working here.' Her eyes fell on a box of contraceptives and she swallowed. He was staring at her, and she was terrified that he could read her mind. Did she have the word written on her forehead? *Pregnant*. She said desperately, 'Have you been working here long?'

'Just a couple of months.' She recognised what was in his eyes then. He was wondering how she would react if he asked her out on a date. He must have decided that she might say yes, because he smiled and said, 'I got a job in Vancouver after I graduated. Then my mom got sick, so I thought I'd better find something closer to home.'

'I'm sorry about your mother.' The test kit was probably something you had to ask the pharmacist for.

There was no way that she could ask here. 'Bad luck,' she added, starting to move away.

'Maybe not,' his voice followed her. 'Right now I think it might have been very good luck—for me.' She shook her head, but couldn't think of any polite words to put him off. In the end she just left without saying anything.

She found it in the second chemist. It was boxed in a largish container, sitting innocently on a display at the back of the store near the prescription counter. The pharmacist that belonged behind this counter was mercifully absent and Mary stood in the aisle, staring at the display and reading the words on the boxes.

Reliable, said the box. Results in one hour. Beta test—whatever that was. The words 'Home pregnancy test' were the ones that shouted out at her. What if she picked up the box and went up to the counter and found herself staring at someone from the choir, or a girl from the young people's group? She would pass the box over, and before ringing the numbers into the cash register the assistant would look at the box. Then look at Mary.

And there wasn't any other reason for having the box, was there? She couldn't say, 'I'm just doing research for a book. You see, I have this character in my new book who thinks she might be pregnant, but she can't go and tell her doctor or have a test at the hospital, so she goes into the store and buys——'

No one would ever believe that. No one would even believe that she was writing a book. Damn! Could the whole thing be her imagination? Sam, it really was—it was wonderful, but we shouldn't have done it. I shouldn't have done it. Look what's happened now!

Or had it happened?

Empty handed, she walked along the aisle until she could see the cash register near the door. The woman at the checkout was someone she had never seen before, and when she asked, 'Yes?' Mary could tell that she wasn't recognised.

'Just looking,' she said, turning back. It was the best chance she would ever have. The store was empty, and the woman had no idea who she was. So there wouldn't be any gossip, and— What if she paused before bagging the box, reading the label, and looking at Mary——

Someone had come into the store, a woman in a shapeless dark coat. Mary had seen a glimpse of the coat, then the top of a dark head of hair moving rigidly along the next aisle. The head had stopped, probably looking at the magazines. The book rack was somewhere close to the dark head.

It was impossible to see the checkout counter from the magazine section. Mary picked up one of the boxes quickly, then grabbed desperately as the whole pile threatened to topple. She had a horrifying certainty that all two hundred or so pregnancy test kits would come tumbling noisily to the floor, bringing everyone running.

They would stand there, the dark woman and the assistant, staring at the minister's daughter caught with the evidence in her hand. Her heart slowed slightly as the boxes stabilised under her desperate fingers. If there had been noise, it couldn't have been much. She waited, breathless, but the dark head was still bent over something in the next aisle.

Get it over with. Hurry!

She picked up the box and walked quickly, thankful for her silent, rubber-soled running shoes. The woman at the cash register didn't even seem to see the writing on the box. She frowned at the numbers on the price sticker, punched in the price, her long, bright red fingernails clicking on the keys of the cash register. Eleven dollars. It seemed wrong somehow that something this crucial, this frightening, could be purchased for only eleven dollars.

She fumbled for change, had a terrifying moment when she couldn't find anything but a five-dollar note. She would have to write a cheque, and that meant identification, recording her name for this woman to remember.

Footsteps behind her. Why didn't the assistant put the damned box in the bag? Mary yanked at a piece of paper in her wallet. A ten-dollar note went floating down to the floor and she bent after it, coming back up in a hurry and pushing the two notes across the counter. The box was sitting there, screaming its purpose for anyone who cared to read it. And behind her——

'Mary, there you are! I wanted to tell you——'

She swung around, and attempted to stand between Emily Derringer and that horrible box on the counter. Emily's hazel eyes were trying to look around Mary. The assistant had paused, money in her hand, and it might be forever before the box got safely into an anonymous paper bag.

'Emily,' she gasped, trying to think of something distracting to say. The older woman was looking at her now, her eyes sharp with accusation. Mary tried to tell herself that she always looked like that. Of all people to run into right now! Emily had a magazine in her hand, and she was waiting for the checkout herself. She moved slightly to one side. Mary moved with her, blocking her view. 'You were going to tell me something?'

'Yes, a message for your mother, it was——' Emily put a cautious hand to her rigidly sprayed hair just as Mary heard the wonderful sound of a stapler on the bag.

'Mother's expecting me home with this parcel.' Mary's words rushed out. 'And I—— Look, why don't you telephone your message to Mother? She'll be home this evening.'

The package was too large to fit into her bag. She put it into the carrier of her scooter and got away from the chemist as fast as she could. Emily was probably still standing there, telling the assistant all about Mary and the Houseman family. Damn! It was her own fault. How could she have been so insane as to think she could behave like one of her own characters when she met Sam?

There was no car in the driveway at the parsonage, nobody in the big old house. She ran up to her room and tore open the bag. The instructions said to do the test first thing in the morning, but she couldn't wait that long. It was bad enough waiting an hour for the results. She followed the directions carefully, set up the vials in her cupboard. That way, if anyone came into her room she could close the door, and they wouldn't know that there was anything at all going on. It was almost as safe as putting her fantasies on to computer disk, because her mother had an active dislike of computers.

She would never put a heroine in a situation like this!

CHAPTER THREE

MARY pedalled hard, trying to make the crest of the hill without having to get off the bicycle and walk. On the other side, the road stretched down gently in a long slope. She coasted, squeezing the brake controls gently with her hands to control her speed as she rolled silently, quickly down the hill, then leaning into the curve as the crescent bent around the contours of Hospital Hill, her hair streaming out behind her.

She had left the church an hour ago, slipping away early for her appointment, needing this time alone, trying still to take in the incredible reality. She was going to have a baby. Right now it was her secret, but this secret was a time bomb. Sooner or later, like that book that would one day go to press, the baby would become a public reality.

Even the idea of Mary Houseman being pregnant was impossible. She shuddered at what her mother would say, but even worse was the thought of her father. It would be in his eyes. Sometimes he looked at her as if he was worried, as if he did not understand her, and she knew what he was thinking. Would she disappoint him, as Toby had? He was a clergyman, leading his flock, but his own family must be above reproach.

There was another possibility, but it seemed as inconceivable as having a baby. She couldn't help thinking about it, but she didn't think she could do it. Abortion. The only way to keep her secret, but ... The whole thing was impossible ... unless Sam was at her side. What if she went back to Vancouver, back to the beach where

she had met him. Would he ever go back? Looking for
Alex? Would he...want her? Want the child? She closed
her eyes in a brief, painful spasm. The child. A baby.
She had not let herself think of it as a baby, a live thing.
She could not afford to let herself think that way,
unless——

She would have liked to go down to the bus station
and catch a Greyhound going anywhere, or to the ferry
terminal and ride to the Queen Charlotte Islands, walk
among the trees out there and forget everyone. Instead,
she rode her bicycle to her appointment.

Outside the clinic she saw a white Corvette, and
wondered if her heart would stop every time she saw a
car like his. She bit her lip, went in and announced herself
to the receptionist. 'Five minutes,' promised Mrs
Bramley, running her hand through the hair that escaped
her nurse's cap. 'You'll not have to wait more than five
minutes.'

'Thanks.' Mary sat down beside an old man, picked
up a magazine and opened it randomly. She stared at
the print as it swam out of focus. The man beside her
shifted a little, as if to read over her shoulder. When the
words came clear in front of her eyes, she found herself
reading an article on nutrition for expectant mothers.

A nurse she didn't recognise came to the waiting-room,
and gestured to the man leaning over her shoulder. 'Dr
Dempsey will see you now, Mr Parker.' Soon Dr Box's
nurse came and Mary swallowed a lump of tears as she
followed the white uniform down the corridor. Then she
was safe, inside the office, and the door was shut behind
her. Dr Box was there, and he handed her a tissue without
asking any questions, then busied himself with writing
something until she was in control of herself again.

'Did you come in for a talk?' he asked mildly as he
looked up.

A talk? She nodded, gulped, and got the words out. He took it calmly, wanted to know the brand of the test that she had bought in the chemist. He examined her and it seemed that there was no doubt at all. They talked and she tried to sound calm and very practical, but inside she was frantic, then numb. She tried to focus on his words as they seemed to spin into nonsense, sounds without meaning. She couldn't have been in his office for more than fifteen minutes, and she left with a slip of paper, and she still didn't know what she was going to do, what she could do. All the possibilities seemed—*impossible*!

They had talked about her options. *Options!* None of them were possible! Have a baby, here, with everyone she knew watching, her parents pained and hurt and ashamed of her. Or... She didn't know who had brought up the other option, herself or Dr Box. He had placed a telephone call, then given her that slip of paper with the address and an appointment time. She stared at it now, already crumpled in her hand, and it seemed like something in someone else's book. A fantasy. A story. Fiction. Impossible that it had been *her* voice inside that office, saying yes, she had enough money in her savings account, and yes, she could get to Vancouver for that day.

Across the corridor an office door was open, the inside of the office a little disorganised as it would be if a new man was settling in. The new doctor, she remembered absently. The other doors were closed. Behind her, Dr Box's door was closed, too. She felt odd, light-headed, and wondered if she was going to faint. A nurse walked past, stared at her curiously. Mary started to move. She had to get out of here. If she stood around, looking shocked, someone was going to wonder. If Emily

Derringer heard about it, Mary wouldn't be surprised if she guessed at the truth.

She had to go somewhere she could be alone. So many secrets. Her writing. Sam. Being...pregnant. How on earth had she got into such a horrible situation?

A door opened beside her and she stumbled, changing course to dodge a pair of long, muscular legs clad in grey. The legs paused. A man's voice said, 'Be sure to give me a call if there's no improvement within forty-eight hours.'

Her eyes flew from the grey slacks to the dark face. Sam? Sam in a suit? Her eyes, wide and startled, met his. Both pairs of brown eyes reflected shock and alarm.

'What are you doing here?' he demanded. Unwillingly, but irresistibly, his hand moved to her arm. She looked down at the paper in her hand, her fingers closing, crushing it into the cup of her palm.

'Alex?'

She shook her head. All her life she had hidden her thoughts, told little untruths to keep things smooth, but at this moment she could not think of one word, neither lie nor truth.

'Something's wrong,' he said grimly.

She seemed unable to pull away when he gripped her arm harder. He pulled her across the hall and into the office, the messy one, dragging her along with him like a rag doll. He shoved the door shut and the noise echoed, emphasising their isolation from the rest of the clinic. 'What are you doing here?' she whispered. In the office, the telephone on the desk was ringing. He picked it up, said abruptly, 'Hold my calls. I don't want to be disturbed.'

His calls? She looked around, and realised that the office was even more of a mess than she had thought at first. On the floor behind the desk were stacks of books.

The desk was piled with files. Behind the desk, the window looked out on the harbour. On the wall there was a pale spot where there had been a painting once. There were diplomas hanging there. Her eyes read words attesting to the qualifications of Samuel Dempsey, doctor of medicine.

Sam. Samuel Dempsey. Her eyes were drawn to him unwillingly. He was standing behind the desk, his fingers still resting on the telephone, darkly bleak eyes watching her assessment of the room.

'You're a doctor?' She knew the answer. 'The new doctor?'

He didn't smile. He said, 'A shock, isn't it? I never dreamed this was your northern town.'

So he hadn't wanted to find her here. She swallowed. 'Why did you come?' The breath went short in her lungs. 'Why here?'

'Fate, I guess.' He didn't sound very happy about it. 'I was ready to leave the hospital, and Roy Box was down south looking for someone.' He shrugged. 'You'd better tell me your name, hadn't you? And why you were looking like that out in the hallway?'

'Mary,' she said slowly. She swallowed, added, 'Houseman.' To gain time, she asked, 'Looking like what?'

'Desperate,' he said harshly.

She shook her head. 'No.'

'Yes. I saw your eyes. You'd better tell me, Alex. You'll have to tell me. I thought—I thought you came here to see me, but you didn't know, did you?'

'No.' She shook her head vigorously. 'I didn't know who you were.' She was going to have to tell him. He could find out anyway. He could ask Dr Box, or go and look in her file—— No, it wasn't in her file, was it? Dr Box had said—— Perhaps Sam needn't know. If he were her lover, loving her, she could tell him and it would be a joy, a gift to them both. But he didn't want her here, in his new town, and she didn't think she could bear to watch his eyes if he learned the truth.

'Alex?'

'It's Mary.' She shivered. Her legs were trembling. Weakness, perhaps, because she had not eaten lunch.

He grinned, and for a second she saw the man on the beach, the man who had been her lover. 'I can't possibly call you Mary.' In his eyes was the memory of how his caresses had driven her to wild abandon. 'It will have to be Alex.'

'Well, for heaven's sake, don't call me Alex in front of Emily Derringer.' She was amazed to hear her own laughter. 'She'll never stop asking about it!'

'Sit down, Alex. You're trembling like a leaf.' He moved towards her, as if he would push her into the straight-backed chair that was sitting there. She sat quickly and he retreated, leaning his hips back against the desk, his arms crossed and his legs stretching out a little towards her.

'You look different,' she said nervously, her eyes following the crisp crease of his slacks, down to the polished black of his shoes.

'So do you.' In Vancouver she had been wearing a very elegant suit. He had been dressed in blue jeans. Now she was in jeans and a cotton blouse, while he sported an expensive grey suit.

'You'd look better in brown,' she said abruptly. 'The grey makes you look pale.' She looked down at her own hands twisting the slip of paper into a mangled ball.

'Tell me what's worrying you, Alex? Why are you here? To see Roy?' She was silent. He frowned. 'You're not sick, are you?'

'No,' she admitted, although she had told Mrs Bramley that it was probably the flu. She spoke in a rush, 'I'm really all right and—and you don't need to worry about it. Don't you have patients waiting?'

'I want the truth, Alex.' She couldn't hold his gaze, those dark eyes penetrating as if he had a right to know whatever was inside her. It was unsettling, scary.

'The truth?' she whispered.

He nodded. 'Lie to anyone else you want, but not me.'

She heard a voice outside, but no one knocked on this door. If they did, he would send them away. She stared at her hands, at the scrap of paper crumpled under her fingers, the faint black smear from her bicycle chain. She was terrified. More than anything else she wanted to get out of here, away from him. She realised that she really was a terrible coward. She hadn't the guts to tell anyone the truth about anything.

His hand covered hers, turned and clasped her fingers with his, the roughness soothing against her cool skin. The paper dropped into her lap. She picked it up with her free hand and held it out to him. He let her hand go, and she saw that his fingers were trembling as he smoothed the slip of paper to read it, as if he was afraid of what he would see.

She watched his face grow very still, her hands clasped together tightly. Would he know what the address meant? Did he know the name of the clinic, know——? What would he feel? What if——? What if he thought that it was some other man's child? No, surely he must know. He was the only person in the world that she might be able to talk to about it, but she was terrified of what he would say, would feel.

He turned away before she could see his eyes. She watched him walk towards the window, staring out, his jaw rigid.

'Sam?' she whispered.

'You—— You're—expecting a child?' His voice was choked.

She nodded but he could not see, looking out, so she said, 'Yes.' There was a long moment without words. Finally she said, 'Sam, I know you're not—I don't expect anything from you or—— I——'

'Stop it, Alex!' For the first time she was actually physically frightened of him, unsure of what he might do. He looked as if he wanted to strike her. There was a sharp knock on the door behind her.

'Dr Dempsey?' Sam didn't seem to hear it. Mary knew that she couldn't possibly stay here, could not face his anger and whatever he had to say to her. She stumbled to her feet and reached the door.

'Alex?'

She froze, her fingers on the knob, then she opened the door and escaped, slipping past the startled nurse. Sam made no attempt to follow her. He stared at the nurse, not seeing her.

'Doctor, the next patient is waiting.' She had the chart in her hand and he took it, nodding curtly, but when the nurse was gone his eyes went back to the crumpled slip of paper he had taken from Alex.

When she had offered the paper to him, he had had a moment of terrified panic, imagining her ill with some terrible disease. Like an unknowledgeable, panicky layman, he had thought instantly of cancer. Surely not Alex! She had been surging through and through with healthy young life, and he'd been suddenly terrified that she was going to be struck down, hurt and helpless.

He had recognised the name of the clinic written in Roy's ragged handwriting. The clinic was new to Vancouver. There had been a good deal of controversy over its establishment, but it provided a competent medical service, and if he had felt the need to refer a patient out of town for an abortion he would probably have made the same decision that Roy had.

He felt as if someone had hit him in the stomach, hard. He stared at the paper, knowing that he must go to the waiting patient, trying to give his face time to grow a mask back. He remembered her white skin under his body, her fingers clenched in his hair, her eyes wide and vulnerable beneath him. A baby, growing inside her, his seed despite the precautions. Swelling the firm white abdomen, filling her face and her breasts and . . .

He looked down at the paper in his hand. Next week. Wednesday. Medically it was perfectly safe. An early pregnancy. His mind made an automatic calculation. A little more than five weeks. He tried to adjust his mind to a clinical detachment but he felt nauseated, panicked as if something terrifying was about to happen. He didn't understand the feelings surging up in him, but he knew that he would have to deal with them. Later.

He pushed the paper into his pocket, opened the patient file in his other hand and glanced through it as he walked to the examining-room. It was a thick file. The man had recurring problems with arthritis, yet he couldn't tolerate the anti-inflammatory drugs that had been prescribed.

How would Alex explain another trip to the big city? Another college friend? Alex, touching him, that smile on her lips. Alex, her body soft and welcoming under his, then rigid and swept with passion as he took her, made her his as if it were for an eternity.

Alex and her secrets. Now she had one secret more to keep. His baby growing inside her. He had never contemplated fathering a child. His child. It haunted him all day, and, when the office visits were over, he sat alone in his office for a long time before he went to the appointment book.

It was there, written in under Roy's three-thirty slot. Mary Houseman. He went to the card file, found the address, then went out and sat in his car for a long time before starting the engine.

He found the house. It was rambling and attractive, but probably poorly insulated. He pulled up in the driveway, rapped on the heavy wooden door and heard the sound echoing. He wondered what he was going to say, and when she opened the door and stared up at him with wide, frightened eyes he still did not know what words to use.

'Alex, I've got to talk to you.'

She swallowed, looking up at him. He was large and muscular and too close. She nodded, tried to smile. His hands hung by his sides and she could see the fingers curled into fists. The lines of his face were deep and harsh. She could feel the frigid outside air radiating from his jacket. He was still dressed like a doctor, formally. From the look of him, he'd come to add to her problems, not to solve them.

'Sam, I—we can't talk here. My father's here.'

Thank heaven her mother was out! Mother would be hovering, wanting to know everything about this man. He was cold and hard. Mary could not imagine how she could have lain intimately against his body, touching and making formless sounds as he caressed her.

She glanced back at the living-room. 'I don't——'

'Just get your damned coat and come with me!' She stared at him, swallowed something hard and dry. He reached out an impatient hand, pulled down a white coat from the cupboard near the door.

'No, that's my mother's. Sam, I——' She met his angry eyes. 'I'll come.' She bit her lip and pushed back her hair, but the soft tendrils promptly escaped again. She called into the living-room, 'Dad, I'm just going out for coffee with a friend. I'll be back in about half an hour.'

She left quickly, before her father could ask any questions. Sam's car was parked behind her father's Volkswagen. It was not locked. She opened the passenger door and got in, careful not to watch Sam as he slid into the driver's seat beside her. He didn't start the engine, just sat silently staring through the window at the back of her father's car.

'My mother will be home any minute.' She chewed on her lip. 'Could we drive somewhere? She has a station-wagon, and she'll want to park here. She'll want to know who you are and what you're doing here with me.'

He said slowly, 'Good grief, anyone would think you were a fifteen-year-old girl. Asking permission and—— Why do you put up with this? Why don't you move out or——?'

'They're my family. I love them.'

His shoulders jerked impatiently. 'That doesn't mean you have to live in their pocket for the rest of your life.' She wanted to ask about his family, but his face was emotionless, rigid. On the beach, last month, she might have asked anyway. If she had, she thought he might have answered.

'Alex, I can't let you abort that baby.' His voice was harsh.

She stared at the house, at her father's car. 'Sam, what am I supposed to do?'

'Have the baby.' Blunt, simple words. His face was in shadow. The dark rigidity of his form forbade any touch, any approach. There was only one way that she could possibly have a baby, one answer that everybody could accept, even Emily Derringer.

'Are you saying you'll marry me?'

She felt his shock, then he said tonelessly, 'I'll help you, of course.' She gulped, closed her eyes in a brief spasm of pain. So much for dreams.

'Sam, you have no idea how impossible it is for me to have——' She sucked in a painful breath. 'The advance for the book—it's not that much, and I don't have a job. My family—oh, lord, Sam!'

'I'll give you money, of course, and—and whatever you might need.' His hand reached out and she jerked away.

'Sam,' she whispered. She felt tears starting, overflowing on to her cheeks. Her arm brushed against her abdomen, and she thought she could feel the fullness there. A life inside her, growing. She fumbled with the latch to the door.

'Alex, listen——'

'I can't.' The tears were making her voice quaver. 'I'm sorry, but I just can't face it all. I'm afraid, and I—I can't!'

She let the door swing closed and stumbled away. She rubbed at her eyes with the sleeve of her jacket. The rough corduroy cut into the tender redness around her eyes. Money, he'd offered, but only one thing could save her from what was ahead: marriage.

She got inside and upstairs. Her privacy was purely temporary. Soon her mother would be home and there would be questions. About Sam. She ran a tub of hot water in the bathroom, the one place where she could lock the door and even her mother would not intrude.

She sank down into the warm wetness and tried to let the water soothe her into a state of half-sleep.

Later, clean and pink from the warm water, she dried herself and dressed in a soft track-suit, warmed by the luxurious green that was a little too elegant for jogging. It had been a gift from Aunt Lexie. She wished that Lexie were here to put the world in perspective.

Lexie. Wild Lexie. Wild Toby.

And now Mary?

The doorbell echoed through the house as she brushed her hair. Footsteps. This old wooden house creaked whenever someone walked into the hallway or down the stairs. She heard the front door opening, heard the sound of her father's voice. She could not hear the words, but the tone was questioning, formal, as if he was talking to a stranger.

Sam's voice. She stared at her hands, knew she must go down to reassure him. She didn't know what she was going to do, but she knew that she would not destroy the life growing inside. He must be upset about the abortion on moral or religious grounds. He rejected any thought of marriage or families, and if a man was that wary of relationships, surely he would not want to become a father?

'Mary!' Her father's voice from downstairs.

Was this how the Christians had felt, walking out into the lion's den? Her legs felt weak as she went down the stairs. One look at Sam's face and she knew that her secret could explode at any minute. She curled her fingers around the banister as if it was something safe to cling to.

Her father was standing beside Sam, but she could see only Sam's eyes, black with what must have been fury, glaring up at her. She almost stumbled, because she couldn't look down, couldn't get free of his eyes, then she was standing on the hardwood floor at the bottom of the stairs.

'Mary, do you know this man?' Oliver Houseman sounded incredulous. He would be seeing not the expensive suit, but the angry eyes, the aggressive stance that seemed to threaten anyone who got in his way. A dangerous man.

With a sense of inevitability she saw the door open behind Sam, saw her mother come in and stop short, eyes wide and curious. 'Yes,' she said dully. 'This is Sam Dempsey.'

Her mother gasped, 'Why, Dr Dempsey! How nice of you to come to make yourself known to us!' She moved in front of Sam and extended her hand, momentarily disconcerted when he ignored the gesture. Her voice took on a frosty note as she said, 'I've been hearing about you. You're setting the town on its ear by standing up for the boy who stole that car.'

Sam's eyes narrowed. 'Small town,' Mary murmured, feeling reality slipping away. 'I told you what it was like.'

He said tightly, 'Come out with me. We have to talk.'

This scene was going to turn into a nightmare. Frances looked from Sam to Mary, startled, and her father said unnecessarily, 'Darling, Dr Dempsey is here to talk to Mary.'

Mary shook her head mutely. She wasn't certain who she was saying no to, but Sam's eyes flashed and she could feel the explosion coming before his voice broke the thick tension.

Sam's anger seemed to fill the small entranceway. He swallowed and for a moment she could see panic in his eyes, then he made a gesture that pushed away both her parents, and said abruptly, 'All right, Alex! You win! We'll get married.'

Frances Houseman's lips were silently forming the word 'married,' but Mary just stared at Sam, confused by the contradiction between his words and his voice.

'That's the price, isn't it?' he demanded harshly.

She closed her eyes, shutting out Sam's tense face, her father's confused concern, her mother's shocked gasp. She was far too frightened of what he might say next to appreciate her mother's unusual silence. 'Alex!' he demanded, and she had to open her eyes and meet his. She stepped back, coming against the telephone table and stopping to keep from falling. Sam moved with her, holding her eyes, ignoring the panic in hers.

She pressed her body back against the table, away from Sam. How many people had she seen in the parish, men and women tied together by an unplanned, unwanted pregnancy, fighting each other over the years, tearing their children apart? She had always believed that forced marriages were punishment for the child, not security. If Sam had wanted her, had shared her fragile fantasy...

'Alex, I won't let you go to Vancouver next week.' His words echoed.

She whispered, 'No,' agreeing.

Perhaps he had not heard her. His voice was hard. 'I'll do whatever it takes.' She pushed a hand through her hair, her eyes moving desperately from Sam to her mother who was watching with predatory curiosity, and to her father who seemed to hover between worry and distress.

'Mary, what——' Her mother's voice broke off in a sharp squeak. Mary wondered wildly if a screaming fit might get her out of this. Sam was going to tell her parents that she was pregnant and planning to have an abortion. Then he'd probably put the lid on it by telling them about her book, although that hardly seemed to matter at the moment.

'Dr Dempsey, why are you calling my daughter Alex?' Her father's voice had the tones of a bewildered academician.

'That's how she introduced herself to me.'

Her mother said sharply, 'Why? When?'

Mary pushed her hands through her hair frantically, stepped towards her mother with some vague hope of getting her out of the room, getting her away from Sam. Far away. But it was too late.

'In Vancouver,' Sam said, as if it didn't matter. 'Last month.'

Her father asked distinctly, 'Mary, exactly what is going on around here?'

She didn't know what to say, how to say it. She swung on Sam. 'Why did you have to come here and make everything so damned difficult? Damn it, Sam!' She could hear own voice raised in a scream, but could not seem to stop it. 'You've got no right to come in here and mess up my life! Will you get out of here? Please!'

'As far as making things difficult goes, I had help.' He sounded coldly amused. She shuddered, knowing that she could not stop his words. He continued, 'And there's no point screaming, throwing blame. Neither one of us is to blame for——' he shrugged '—for an equipment failure.'

Equipment failure! Equipment! Her mother's lips opened and Mary said rigidly, 'I simply cannot handle this. I don't know how to handle this!' Sam was staring at her, waiting for something. She screamed, 'Damn you, Sam!'

He would seem relaxed to a casual observer, but she could see the rigid tension in him. His voice was hard. 'Alex, I think it's time you grew up and faced the music. You——'

'No! Sam! Don't——'

'You've gotten into a situation that you can't hide from. This is one secret too many, Alex.'

She shuddered, found herself screaming, 'Sam! Go away! Get out! I'm not ready to face this!'

A muscle twitched in his jaw. The scar stood out red and angry on his cheekbone. His brown eyes deepened almost to black, hiding his deepest thoughts from her. Then, abruptly, the tension seemed to flow out of him. He pulled a pen from his inside jacket pocket, stepped over to the telephone table and wrote briefly on a piece of paper. Everything was deathly silent as he placed the paper in her hand and closed her fingers on it.

'When you're ready to talk, come and see me. Or call.' She swallowed, remembering the other paper with the address. He had never given it back to her. Now he said insistently, 'Promise me that, Alex?' She nodded, and he didn't say goodbye to her, or her parents. He just left her alone, standing in the midst of a silence that didn't last long enough, the sound of the door slamming behind him echoing through the old house.

Her father began in his pastor's voice, 'Mary, I think——'

Her mother overrode his quiet concern with, 'Mary Alexandra, I think you'd better tell us what this is all about! This man—— My goodness, Emily led me to believe he was a reasonable—a normal—— Mary, what on earth do you have to do with him?'

Mary felt numbed. What else could happen? Exhausted from the tension of waiting for Sam to expose her secret, she found herself blurting, 'I'm pregnant.' She felt a relief as the words came out, and added flatly, 'He's the father.'

Her father swung around. His eyes went to Frances for guidance. Her mother's mouth opened soundlessly. Her eyes were dark and shocked, then she managed a choked, 'Oh, no, Oliver! Didn't we go through enough with Toby?' Mary heard the words and wondered where all her feelings were hiding. 'A baby?' Her mother's words were tight and painful. 'He—Dr Dempsey——?' She heard her mother swallow. 'He's the father? He's the man who——?'

She didn't answer. What could she say? She stared at the door and knew that she had to get away from this. Her mother took a deep breath, and licked her lips. 'You've always had that streak in you,' she said sadly. 'Just like your brother. Just like Lexie, too. She was a wild girl, and she's a wild woman. I've tried to make sure you didn't grow up like them. I knew it was in your blood.'

Frances reached a frantic hand up to her hair, but hesitated short of actually disturbing the immaculate *coiffure*. 'Don't you realise what this means? Can you imagine how your father will face this? His daughter! We are the clergy, we set an example, show others how—— Oh, my goodness! Mary, this is absolutely impossible!'

Mary had never in her life walked away from Frances when she was throwing a tantrum, but she found that her legs would move. Frances screamed, 'He asked you to marry him! I heard him! He——'

That's the price, isn't it? His words echoed with all their anger. To him it was a trap, and she was not tempting bait. Her hands found the doorknob.

'It's dark! You can't go out this time of——'

She dodged her mother's restraining hand, then the door was shut and she was outside. The darkness flowed over her like a conealing blanket. Her feet took her down the hill. It was easier than going up.

She walked for a long time without knowing where she was or what her thoughts were. Eventually, she realised that the night was growing cold, that her jacket was back at the house. She had come to the waterfront, walking down and down the hills like water seeking its level. There was no pavement here on the waterfront road, and from time to time the taxis roared past with their lights on high-beam and their wheels burning up the tarmac.

She had nowhere to go, but could not face going back to her parents. She had no idea what she could say to her mother, how she could face the words and the questions, much less the shock and recriminations. Once, when she was seventeen, she had gone out with a young man who had held her and had kissed her, and had somehow touched the needs inside her. He had wanted her, and she had felt desire, too. He had kissed her lipstick away, had touched her breasts with heated yet gentle hands, and had made her tremble with her own feelings, before her inhibitions had finally regained control and she had pushed him away. It was the closest she had ever come to a woman's passion, until Sam.

When she had arrived home that night, her mother had been waiting, and her eyes had fixed on Mary's flushed young face, seeing too much in the wide eyes and the swollen lips. There had been questions and accusations, a long, painful scene in the living-room while her father had slept upstairs. The ghost of Toby's wildness, his suicide. The shadow of an irresponsible Aunt Lexie.

She had never gone out with him again.

She stopped in the light from a street-lamp and pulled a crumpled piece of paper out of her pocket. A hotel room number, a pager telephone number. An angry Sam seemed a doubtful refuge. She felt exposed, remembering how she had lain with him, how she had reached out to touch him, feeling his innermost self responding to her exploration. How could he have been so close then, yet such a harsh stranger now?

The end of the road. She had reached the floats where the fishing boats and pleasure craft were moored. The waterfront car park was half-full. She stopped at the pier and leaned against the rail, looking down as a boat went past outside the breakwater logs, roaring in the dark. In its wake, the waves worked their way under the logs and the boats began to move, setting up a strange, disjointed rhythm amid a chorus of metallic clanging and wooden squeaking. She saw no one, not a single soul, although there must be people somewhere down there.

She went down the ramp, held on to the cold metal rail. There was no one in the world as she made her way along the floats. Why had she come here? She arrived finally at the last finger, at a beautiful house built of cedar, mounted on a new steel barge. She had never been inside it, but it belonged to Maggie and Michael MacAvoy.

Maggie was the harbour manager. She had lived down here on the docks with her daughter for four or five years, and Mary knew her to talk to. Sometimes, when interesting things happened down here, Maggie would telephone and Mary would have material for her next column. A few years ago Mary had been at home from university for the summer, and she had heard the whispering as her parents had talked about Maggie, the woman who had left her worthless husband, and had struck out alone with her young daughter and no resources, no way to make a living. Maggie had survived that, had found a job and had managed to support herself and her daughter. Then, last year, she had married Michael MacAvoy.

Mary admired Maggie MacAvoy, but they weren't intimate friends, surely not close enough for Mary to come knocking on Maggie's door in the middle of the night when the windows were all dark.

CHAPTER FOUR

THE fire in the MacAvoys' living-room was crackling with warmth, the flames licking softly over the driftwood as it burned. Michael had lit it, then he had kissed his wife, smiled at Mary, and returned to bed.

Maggie made coffee, delivering it with a grin and a toss of her coppery curls. 'Don't worry, it won't keep you awake. Michael can't stand decaffeinated, but I drink it in the evening. Here, pull your chair a little closer to the fire.'

Maggie, sitting quietly, was easy to talk to. It was a side to the wharfinger that Mary had not seen before. Normally she saw Maggie in motion, organising boats, dealing with difficult skippers, working hard. 'I don't really know what I'm doing here. I just—— Somehow I landed up at your door, knocking. I don't know why.'

Anyone else would be asking questions. Maggie didn't. 'Have your coffee, and relax. There's a bed in the spare room if you're tired. If you want to talk, I'm here; or, if you prefer, you're welcome to the bed without the talk.'

Mary pushed back her brown hair, tucking the waving tendrils behind her ear. She said slowly, 'I met a man.'

'That does complicate life, doesn't it?' Maggie was smiling as her eyes went to the stairs leading up to the room she shared with Michael.

'Not like you and Michael,' Mary said in a rush. 'Michael loves you. But Sam—I met him last month. I was in Vancouver for two days for...' She hesitated, then everything came out. The book. The publisher. Sam.

64

The baby. When the words were all said, the room filled with the warm sounds of the fire.

'I liked him,' said Maggie when the silence had grown comfortable. 'I was at the clinic earlier this week. I had an appointment with Dr Box, but he was called out and the new doctor took my appointment.' Amazingly, Maggie blushed. 'I'm expecting a baby, too. You're the first to know, except Michael and Dixie, of course. I just learned yesterday. I liked Dr Dempsey very much. You've got yourself quite a man.'

Mary shook her head. 'I haven't. We don't have a relationship. There was just the—the one night. It was never supposed to be more than that, not for either of us. And when he came back and said he would marry me, it was—he talked as if it was a punishment!' She brushed moisture away from her eyes.

'Hung up about family life, I suppose,' said Maggie. 'But then, we all are, aren't we? After my divorce, I thought I'd never get involved again. I almost threw away the best thing that ever happened in my life before Michael got through to me.' Maggie grinned and said warmly, 'Do you mind if I call you Alex? I have to admit that I agree with Sam. You're much more an Alex than a Mary.'

'It's a dangerous name, though.' She smiled wryly, her eyes narrowing on the fire. 'It makes me feel like someone else, reckless. It's my middle name, after my Aunt Lexie—that's short for Alexandra.'

Maggie tossed back curls and stared intently at Mary, as she said slowly, 'It seems to me that in all of this the real problem is your trying to please other people. Hadn't you better make your decisions for yourself and the baby, and forget about the rest of them? Take some time alone, decide what you're going to do, then come out of hiding and ask Sam or your parents for help if you need it.'

Money, Sam had offered. She walked to the window, staring out. The warm easiness of Maggie's home was an uncomfortable contrast to what would be waiting for her at home. 'My mother's waiting. Sam's waiting, too. I'm supposed to call him, or go to see him. And I don't know what to say to either of them. Right now I feel as if they're all tearing me apart.'

'You're exhausted. You can't possibly make any sensible decisions when you're so tired.' Maggie stood up.

'I have to——'

'You don't have to do anything. Not until you've had a sleep. There's a bed right there, through that door. You go in there, and I'll bring you a nightgown you can use.' Maggie walked across and opened the bedroom door. 'It's my father-in-law's room, but he's away right now. Go to bed and have a good sleep. There's nothing that can't be settled easier after you've slept.'

'I can't, Maggie.' She raked her hands through her hair, and said regretfully, 'My mother will be frantic, wondering where I am. The longer I am, the worse it will be. And if I try to call, she'll come here. You don't know her. She——'

Maggie shook her head vigorously, her legs moving astride and her hands settling on her slender hips. 'Bed! Now!' Her voice was snapping out instructions as if no one could dare argue. 'You don't have to face anybody until you're ready. That room is yours as long as you need it, and I can guarantee you that no one will disturb you there until you're prepared to be disturbed.' Mary's lips parted and Maggie said sharply, 'I'll call your mother.'

Maggie MacAvoy was only about five feet four, but Mary had heard tales of her facing down angry men here on the docks, and no one told any stories where Maggie came out the loser. Like everyone else, Mary lost out in the face of Maggie's charm and determination. She found herself in old Angus MacAvoy's empty bedroom, dressed in a filmy green nightgown that probably made Maggie's green eyes glitter as if she were an enchanting sorceress.

Somehow, amazingly, she slept almost the instant her head hit the pillow. When she woke, the sun was shining on to her face. She lay quietly, listening to the sounds of this house. Dixie's high-pitched voice. Michael laughing, Maggie joining him.

There hadn't been any answers in her sleep, but she had lost that frantic need to run, to get away from what was happening. It was real, here, and somehow she would find her way.

It was incredible that Mary Alexandra Houseman, after twenty-five years of living as the model child, the model daughter, had managed to get into a situation where she was bound to create nothing but pain and controversy. She was a good girl, an obedient girl, a girl who never got into trouble. Not like her younger brother who had gone from drinking to drugs and finally suicide. Not like the Onhousers' daughter who used to cuddle in the back seats of cars, parking up on Hospital Hill in the camp-ground. She had gone away for a year at the age of sixteen, returning looking older and sadder. Not like Harriet Westlake who had married Jeremy Columbia and left school to have twins. Last week Harriet had been crying in their living-room, because she was twenty-six now and she had five children and a husband who did not love her.

Mary had stayed out of trouble for a quarter of a century and it had not been hard, not until the night she'd decided to call herself Alex.

Maggie was right. She could not deal with this pregnancy the same way she had dealt with all the other problems in her life. Trying to avoid making waves, to maintain everyone's good opinion of her. What would Maggie do in a situation like this? Maggie had had the courage to walk away from a hopeless marriage, to look after herself and her child alone. Did Alex have the courage to do that? Did she want to? Alex, she thought with an odd sense of amusement, I'm thinking of myself as Alex. She made a mental decision to adopt the name, and the personality that went with it. It seemed appropriate.

In a terrible sense, she was now free to choose her own path. She had already hurt her parents. Now that she had told them she was pregnant, there was no solution to her pregnancy that they could accept without problems. As for Sam, she suspected that the answers to Sam's reactions lay in his own past, and she doubted if he would ever share that with her.

She heard someone taking a shower. Maggie's voice, then Dixie's, higher pitched, and Michael's laughter again. Love flowed everywhere in this home. A door slammed, then opened again immediately and Maggie called out, 'Dixie! Come back! You forgot your lunch!' A telephone rang, twice. Alex tensed, heard Maggie's voice, low and determined, but could not make out the words. She expected someone to call her to the telephone, but moments passed and there was nothing but the sound of the water tap again, then low conversation between Maggie and her husband.

There were things she had to do. She wondered idly where the MacAvoys got their water with their house out here on the wharves. She closed her eyes and, somehow, drifted back into a state of half-wakefulness. She jerked awake when the door opened.

'Sorry,' said Maggie, slipping into the room with a steaming mug in her hand. She was wearing blue jeans, a denim jacket and sturdy running shoes. 'Did I frighten you? I didn't want to knock and wake you up if you were sleeping. I brought you coffee, with caffeine this time! I'm just heading off to check the boats. I'll be back in a couple of hours. Meanwhile, make yourself at home. I unplugged the telephone, so no one will bother you.'

Alex shifted herself up against the pillows. 'I should get up.'

'No need. Relax and enjoy being alone. It seems to me you're hardly ever alone, always having people chasing after you for one thing or another.'

It had always been that way. Her only private life had been in her room, in her fantasies. And once, in Vancouver.

'My mother will call.' It was almost nine o'clock and Alex was amazed that her mother had not yet managed to invade this home. 'She'll wonder, if there's no answer.' It was fine to lie here alone and speculate on a life of her own, but facing the reality of her mother was another thing. 'I'm frightened of her,' Alex said on a note of discovery. 'I've always been terrified of her. I think Dad's terrified of her, too.'

Maggie grinned, her green eyes laughing. 'I'm not. I told her you were sleeping, getting a much-needed rest, and that you would be staying with us for a few days. I told her not to call and not to come; that you needed some time alone and would get in touch when you were ready.'

Alex choked on the coffee. 'I should keep you around, just to deal with my mother.'

'I've been fighting off an overbearing father all my life. I've had practice. Michael keeps me in practice, too. If I don't watch him, he takes over. Do you want me to call Sam?'

Soon she would have to talk to Sam. Tonight, she decided, and Maggie went off to make a call to Sam's office.

It was a strange day for Alex. She spent most of it on the floats, and, although she intended to spend her time thinking, working out her future, most of the time her mind seemed blank. She had lunch alone with Maggie in the beautiful house on the barge. Michael, it seemed, was busy at the site for his new building. He had managed to acquire one of the few waterfront leases and was tearing down the old condemned buildings.

'What's he going to build there?' asked Alex.

'Everything!' Maggie spread her hands. 'It's going to be sort of a drive-in electronics and marine shop for boats.'

'He has an electronics company down south, doesn't he?'

Alex was surprised when Maggie burst out laughing. 'Oh, yes, his corporate empire is down there. Some day I'll tell you about Mickey and me. It was fireworks, from the day Dixie pushed his niece into the ocean until the night of the *tsunami* warning.' Maggie was grinning, remembering. 'Oh, and by the way, Sam said he would come over this evening. About seven.'

Sitting in Maggie's home, it didn't seem quite so shocking that she might have a baby, without running away from Prince Rupert, without getting married. It was the idea of doing it in her parents' home that was impossible. What she needed was her own place. She probably had enough money in her savings account to support herself in a no-frills style for a few months. With that, and the advance that was coming on her book, she might scrape through until the baby came.

But that was no way to bring a child into the world, not knowing where the next dollar was coming from. It would be better if she could find a part-time job that would leave her enough time to get the second book well on its way. But who would want to hire a pregnant woman with a university degree and no experience?

After supper that night, she sat out on the balcony on the second storey, and played three games of draughts with Dixie. 'That's it! I quit,' Alex finally declared. Dixie was grinning, pleased with her victory. Alex said with a laugh, 'You're a menace!'

'It's just that I have a lot of practice,' said the girl with a grin. 'I play with my grandpa all the time. He lives with us, you know, in the room you're using.'

Alex nodded. 'Where is he now?'

'Visiting my aunt.' Dixie was frowning and Alex suspected that the aunt was not a favourite with the girl.

'Dixie! Time to do your homework!' Michael's voice came clearly from below. Dixie grimaced and started putting the draughts away. 'English,' she muttered. 'I've got to do a short story, and I hate writing stories.' The girl ran off, the draughts board under her arm, and Alex watched her going until her eyes were fixed on the man who came through the doorway, stepping aside to let Dixie past. Sam.

She remembered the first time she had seen him. He had seemed dangerous, yet he had drawn her like a magnet. Something in him seemed to touch her where no one else ever had. She knew that she could very easily love this man. She also knew that she must not, because he did not want love. He stood still, his eyes serious and faintly worried, watching her. Then he walked slowly towards her. For a moment she thought he would touch her, but he moved to the rail of the balcony and sat on it with one hip, his leg swinging slightly.

'You look like Sam again.' He was dressed in the familiar jeans, with a casual shirt unbuttoned at the neck.

'I'd dress like this for work,' he said, smiling faintly while his brown eyes remained serious. 'But I guess somewhere inside I'd have trouble convincing myself that I was the doctor and not still a delinquent kid running the streets.' His smile faded and he said, 'You're looking better today, Alex.'

She looked away, trying not to see the caring in his eyes that was somehow mixed with reserve and something else she could not identify. 'I had a good sleep.' Her fingers played with the skirt of the outfit that Maggie had loaned her to wear. The skirt was bright and pretty, matching the embroidered cotton blouse. Alex felt conspicuous in it. 'I've spent most of the day thinking.'

He slipped off the balcony rail and her heart stopped. His hand reached out, the callused warmth touching her cheek, brushing down to touch her lips fleetingly.

'Alex, I—I'm sorry.'

She licked her lips nervously, hoping he could not see what she was feeling. Some perverse part of her wanted to move close, to see if his arms would go around her, if he would touch her and kiss her . . . and need her the way he had the night he became her first lover. Her only lover.

'I got you into this.' He seemed to be having trouble with his breathing. She could see his chest moving, a faint flush on his face. 'This is my fault, my responsibility. I think—the sooner we get married the better it will be. I can see—what with your parents, and the church, and the rest of it—well, it's an impossible situation for you. I can see that. I—I'll look after you, Alex, and the baby.'

Her mouth was dry, her lips seemed to be cracking. She licked them again, unable to look away from him, her heart thundering as an ominous pressure seemed to descend on her.

'I've been looking at houses,' he said, pushing his hands into his pockets, his voice becoming almost toneless. 'I'll buy a house, and we should be able to get married next week. I'll go down and apply for the licence tomorrow. I——'

'Sam!' Her voice echoed sharply. She could see the wharves extending down below the balcony. Below her, a man walking along the float had heard her voice and was looking around in confusion, unable to discern where the sound had come from.

Alex lowered her voice. 'Sam, you weren't the only one responsible for this. You took precautions. And I— I wanted to make love with you.' Love. The word settled over them. She whispered, 'I don't regret it...even now. But—if I weren't pregnant, would you be asking me to marry you?' She knew that he could not lie to her. He shook his head silently and she managed to say steadily, 'Then we can't possibly get married.'

He pushed her words aside with a gesture. 'You're shivering,' he said, as if she were his patient. 'You'd better come into the house.'

'Just nerves. The sun's still out.'

His eyes were on her bent head, following the smooth glossy line of her shoulder-length brown hair, trying to see what she was thinking. Then he stared over the rail at the water below, as if he could see another world in the reflections. 'Alex, it isn't—I never intended to be anybody's father.'

'Why? Sam, you're the father of this child inside me. I—I think I have to understand what you feel about it.'

He pushed unsteady hands through his hair, throwing it into confusion. These were things he never talked about, memories he did not explore and feelings he did not want. He turned to face her, to tell her harshly that she had no right to pry into him or his past. She was sitting very still on the chair, her hand spread over her skirt as if to touch the child inside her. He felt a shuddering wave of emotion surging up over him, equal parts of terror and need.

There were no rings at all on her fingers. Her only jewellery was the gold charm that had hung around her throat from the first time he had seen her. From it her throat rose, soft and smooth and vulnerable. Her face— her lips were slightly parted. He could see the faint pink shadow of her tongue. There was no trace of a smile. The only colour on her face was the faint scattering of freckles across her nose and the dark brown softness that was her hair lying against her cheek and her throat. He felt his hand moving, irresistibly drawn to touch the glossy softness of her hair, her skin. He stopped the motion, his hand clenching.

Finally, inevitably, he looked into her eyes. Framed with long dark lashes, they stared at him. Wide brown eyes, deeper than his could bear to look into. Penetrating too far, seeing too much, yet somehow casting a spell upon him that made it seem as if there was no danger to opening, speaking. 'Alex, I can't exactly explain what I feel.' He heard the huskiness in his voice, and cleared his throat awkwardly.

Her hand caught at his and the brown fingers clenched around hers. She said carefully, her eyes never leaving his, 'Try, Sam. Please.'

He stared at their joined hands. He thought there was no other woman like this in the world, that if he explained she would understand. It would not be easy for him, reaching out, letting another person close, but she would help him, and somehow they would make it all work for the sake of the child. There would be no terror for this child, none of the violence and noise and abuse that had characterised his own youth.

He said slowly, 'I can remember my mother, vaguely. I was with her until I was old enough to go to school, running wild, I suppose. Then somebody decided to investigate why I was on the streets while the other kids were in school. They took me away then, and that's the last time I ever saw her.'

Alex moved her thumb across the hard rigidity of his hand, a soothing touch that he probably did not even notice. How old would he have been? Six? Seven? 'She's just a pretty memory, and not a clear one. Looking back, trying to guess by what I remember, I suppose she was probably making her living as a prostitute. Maybe there were drugs involved. I don't suppose any authority would have considered her a fit mother.'

'What happened to you?'

'Foster homes. I was a difficult little monster, so there were a lot of homes.' He grinned wryly, his hand brushing the hair back from her forehead. 'There's no need to look worried, Alex. I know you can't imagine such an existence with the upbringing you had, but that sort of thing either makes you strong, or it finishes you. I survived it, so I guess it made me strong. I left the last place when I was fourteen.'

Fourteen. Just a child. 'Left, and . . . what?'

He loosened her hand. 'Looked after myself, one way or another. Not always honestly.'

'And you've been alone ever since,' she finished softly.

'I'd had enough of family life. I wanted to make my own rules, my own life, and it wasn't going to include any family. Just me.'

'Sam, it's not always like that.' She stood up and moved to him, her hand resting on his forearm. 'There are lots of exceptions, loving families.'

'I know that.' He looked down at her, his eyes seeming to notice the pretty blouse for the first time, fingers brushing the fabric absently. 'I've made friends, seen enough loving families to know how it can be, but I—— Well, the more I learned, the more it seemed a good idea for me to stay alone.' His fingers stroked her arm, bringing dizzy pleasure to her.

There was a lot missing. 'Somehow you got from that—from the fourteen-year-old street fighter to—Sam, you don't become a doctor by dropping out of school at fourteen.'

'No,' he agreed. 'I racketed around. Then, when I was nineteen, I got caught with a stolen car.' He shrugged that away. 'I didn't much like being in gaol, so I made sure I didn't go back. I managed to find work. Travelling, working—there was lots of work then for a man if he was willing to do anything that took a strong back and gave a pay cheque in return. Picking fruit, working on road crews, fishing.'

'And logging.'

'Yes. That was where the change came. Jake, lord knows why, pulled me out of the bush, went with me when they flew me to Vancouver, made a nuisance of himself at the hospital insisting I have the best care, the best surgeon.' Sam grinned, remembering how unpopular Jake had made himself at the hospital. 'I don't know why he bothered.'

'He cared about you,' said Alex gently.

'I guess.' He obviously wasn't comfortable with that. He shrugged and said, 'I had a long time in there. It was almost a year before I was out and fit to do anything physical again. Quade operated on me, many times. There was quite a bit of pain, but mostly there was time to think, and to watch what was happening around me. I decided that there were better things to do than bumming around. Quade spent a lot of time with me, talking medicine. And Jake kept coming by.' Sam grinned. 'Jake's the kind of guy who can't accept no for an answer. One day I said that I wished I'd finished school, that I would have liked to go to medical school. Within a week Jake had all the information for me, assessment tests set up, information on correspondence and tutors to get my high school diploma. I spent the rest of my hospital stay as a student, trying to catch up on things I hadn't done years before.

'Then I applied for admission to UBC as a mature student.' He smiled at her, a wide amusement. 'I was twenty-eight at the time, so I guess that made me mature enough. The money was a bit of a problem, but it worked out. After the first year, I managed to qualify for the odd scholarship here and there. And there was a settlement for the accident in the bush. Quade got me part-time work as an orderly in the hospital. I made it without starving. Jake had me over for dinner at his place once a week. I don't know if he realised that was about the only balanced eating I got, but I was thankful for it.'

'They both cared a lot about you,' said Alex, not knowing either man, but glad that Sam had not been completely alone all those years.

'I can't think why, but it's true. I probably couldn't have done it without them both behind me.'

'I know why.' She was smiling, a gentle mockery. 'Because you're a very special man, Sam Dempsey. They cared about you because you were worth it, and because you needed it.'

He swallowed, took a deep breath, and said harshly, 'Alex, a man learns how to be a father long before he's a man. He learns by the way he's treated. Kids who come out of unstable environments are likely to repeat history with their own children. I had no notion of having children, and—I—— Then, when I realised that you were carrying my child, I——'

He jerked away from her abruptly and paced across the balcony. His voice had caught, stumbled on his own words, and Alex wasn't sure, but she thought there might have been tears in his eyes. Sam wanted this child. He was afraid of it, but it was a person to him, the child he had never intended to have.

'Sam, you're talking about statistics. You're not a statistic.'

'Yes, I know. Look, Alex, I know I haven't exactly thought of you in all this.' His voice was ragged, his face averted from her. 'I've been sitting at the clinic ever since it closed this evening, trying to think, to be objective, or—well, at least rational. I—damn it, Alex! I really am trying, but all I can see is that it's a baby. It's my baby, Alex! I—what did you say?'

He swung back to face her, his face rigid yet very vulnerable. She wanted to go to him, to touch him and kiss him and tell him that it would be all right, but she knew she must preserve her own composure, must think very clearly.

'Sam, not yours. Ours—no, don't say anything, please! Let me say what I—I've been thinking about this. All day. I've probably had a better chance to think it out clearly, because, thanks to Maggie, I've been all alone most of the day, and no one has been giving me advice—well, except perhaps Maggie, but her advice made sense.'

'What——'

'She said that it was my baby, or my abortion.' His jaw clenched at her words. 'Sam, I'm not going to have an abortion. You don't have to worry about that. But—I feel that we have to be really honest with each other. I don't know if I would have made it down to that clinic in Vancouver if you hadn't found out about it. I—I was scared. I'm still scared, but now I've got to the point where I feel——'

'What are you feeling?' He seemed freed of the forces that had frozen him. He stepped close and touched her face with his hand, gently raising her chin so that he could look into her eyes. Whatever he saw there seemed to affect him strongly. She stared up at him, seeing his pupils widen, the muscles in his throat work as he swallowed. The words seemed drawn from him without his will. 'Alex, it will be all right. I'll—I'll make you a good husband. I'll make sure of that. I—I can see why you might have cause for concern, but——'

'I'm not going to marry you, Sam.' She said it quickly, before she could be tempted by the touch of his fingers on her face, the erotic temptation of his husky male body standing so close to her. Then, as her words echoed around them, she wanted to call them back.

The night she had met him, they had been two souls united, the world only a fantasy around them. It could be like that again. That look was in his eyes, and if she reached out to him as she had before, the rest of the world would fade away. And she would have trapped a man who was filled with gentleness and caring, but terrified of loving. She could feel it whenever he was close to her. He wanted her, had not forgotten their shared ecstasy. Even his eyes answered the deeper messages in hers, but, at the same time, inside him there was anger and resentment at the way she pulled him.

Especially now that she carried his child. There was only one honourable thing that he could do about that knowledge. Marry her. And she was convinced that, despite all that he had lived through, Sam Dempsey was a very honourable man.

He was standing stiffly, his face a mask now as he said rigidly, 'What are you going to do?'

She stood erect and motionless. 'I'm not sure, Sam.'

He said, in a rush, 'Alex, I——'

'No, Sam.' She touched his lips to silence him. His flesh felt warm and dry. 'Don't say anything. There's no hurry to make our decisions. I need time. We both need time. I promise you that I won't do anything that affects this child without telling you, Sam. I won't—there won't be any abortion.' She closed her eyes against his, said raggedly, 'Would you do something for me, please, Sam? Leave me alone now? I have to—I need time.'

'How long?'

'I don't know. A week. A month. I—I just need some time on my own.'

He stared at her wordlessly, then turned away to watch the entrance of a large fishing boat through the break-water. He pushed his hands deep into his pockets before he said carefully, 'No, I can't do that.' She saw his chest expand in a deep breath, heard his voice with the tension in it. 'I can't just walk away and wonder what's happening to you.'

'To the baby, you mean.'

'Both.' His voice was hard. 'You and the baby. You'll just have to put up with me. I'm not going to go away, Alex.'

CHAPTER FIVE

IT WAS as if the town were wrapping its tendrils around Sam. Day by day, he felt himself becoming more deeply entangled into its life.

He was slowly becoming aware of a duality in his role towards his patients. On the one hand he was giving; on the other, hiding emotionally in the safe role of doctor. Although he could be hurt by the pain or death of a patient, his inner self was safe, secure. No person was ever allowed close enough to threaten. It was this distance, this remoteness, that was threatened when he began to feel pressures to move away from hospital life.

Had Alex done something to him in that wonderful night in Vancouver? Had he been altered, somehow drawn into changes, which were restructuring his life, taking it out of his control? Even in the mad days when he ran the streets and took his living where he could find it, he had felt that he was the one in control. It had always been necessary to him, from the moment he walked out of the last foster home, that he have pilotage of his own life, his own destiny. One painful experience with courts and justice had been enough to put him off the streets. *He* must direct his own life, not judges and gaolers beyond his reach.

When he made choices, they were conscious and deliberate. Even becoming a doctor had been a move to gain mastery, of both his own life and the pains of others. He was good at it. When he moved into that world, he felt assurance and something even more. Jake might have called it dedication, a sense of worth, but Sam avoided putting words to it. He simply lived it, refusing to question why.

So here he was, the man who would not put down roots, being insidiously tricked and seduced into accepting the tendrils of commitments. Alex—no, he was not ready yet to come to terms with the whole issue of Alex. He had tried to resolve it quickly, to the inevitable conclusion. It was unfair that Alex should be the one to suffer. He was a man—a doctor, for heaven's sake—yet he had impregnated a virgin. Hell, it was no excuse that he'd taken the usual precautions! He was years older than she, yet he had allowed the mystery in her eyes, the soft trusting touch of her fingers to go to his head. He had been insane to take her, yet he knew that in that same situation, today, he would repeat his insanity. Too many of his dreams were living memories of walking with Alex, talking with Alex, making love.

She might be twenty-five, but she was a child who must be protected. Despite her parents, who seemed to hover so stiflingly close to her, he knew that she lived essentially alone, much as he did. The difference was that her solitary world was one of fantasies where she created stories. Once he realised that she could not stand alone and have the child, he knew that marriage would be the only solution. Not a marriage of passions, but a cool rational arrangement so that he could care for her without having to come too near.

Cool. Rational. In control. Talking with her on the balcony of the MacAvoys' house, he had felt exposed and vulnerable, yet somehow unable to gather defences around him. He wanted to see himself as the strong one, looking after her in her need, without becoming involved himself, but he was aware that his vision of himself was false. His instinct had been to take control once he re-alised that he could not walk away from her predicament, yet Alex would not give him control. So he left her with the MacAvoys, frustrated and uncertain of his own course.

He was just getting into his car in the car park when his pager beeped and a voice echoed through the Corvette, asking him to call the Manor. He telephoned, then went up to spend some time with the Alzheimer's patient. Later, he found himself on maternity. His two mothers were sleeping soundly. He went into the nursery and spent a long time standing there, looking down at the new-borns. General practice was different from hospital life. Too many people. Individuals coming close, pulling in the walls around him. In the hospital he had hidden in surgery, his patients unconscious, or in emergency where they came and went too quickly to break the barriers between Sam and the world. No time, no opportunity to form relationships.

Soon, in mere weeks, a stethoscope placed against the smooth white flesh of Alex's abdomen would allow him to hear the foetal heartbeat. In less than eight months there would be a child. He would be a father.

The nurse was in the next room, changing one of the babies. He was alone with the others; they were mostly sleeping, one husky new-born grinding his fist against his gums. Watching them, Sam felt a sudden clarity of vision.

He was emotionally not much more mature than these new-borns. Afraid to touch, to feel. Fearful of ties and obligations that would twist control away from him. He had held himself aloof, lived in solitary isolation to protect himself. He could choose now. If he was quick and ruthless, he could regain his detachment. Otherwise it would go on, he would become more and more entangled, his life and his happiness dependent on others.

The fears had woken as he moved away from the isolation of institutional life. Logging camps. University dormitories. Hospitals. They were all a way to avoid relationships, personal responsibilities. As he moved away from them, he became more exposed. It was time to grow, he decided as he stared down at a young man who was about to start wailing. Time to change.

Upstairs, Neil MacKenzie was ready to be discharged. Tomorrow morning he would walk out of the hospital, and almost directly into the court-room where he would be charged. Sam had talked to the probation officer and knew that Neil would probably be held in custody until the autumn assizes. The boy had no one to vouch for him, no one rash enough to guarantee behaviour while he waited to be tried. Sam doubted if imprisonment would help the boy, although it might be slightly better than turning him back out on to the streets.

Over at the Manor was the elderly man who had cried on Sam's shoulder only an hour ago, incoherently understanding that he would never be well enough to return to his home, yet worried about his dog. The dog, Sam ascertained with some difficulty, had been left in the care of neighbours. Sam had promised to visit the dog, to make sure he was all right, and the man old enough to be his father had relaxed, trusting the gruff doctor with the scar on his face.

A dog. An old man. A bright young juvenile destined for gaol. A baby not yet born. And Alex...Alex Diamond...Mary Alexandra Houseman. Child-woman with too many secrets. The baby would need a father. He was wary of her, unsure of her plans and uncertain of being able to influence them. Tonight she had understood some of what he felt. Surely she would not keep him from the child, yet——

He picked up the infant as it started to cry. The unsteady head floundered against his shoulder, seeking instinctively for its mother's breast. He staggered slightly under a powerful vision of Alex, his baby suckling at her breast, her head bent to watch the infant, her hair sweeping over her face, touching the child as it rummaged against her.

I love her, he realised with wonder, then pushed away the realisation in panic. No! What could a man with his background know about love? The patterns for relationships were formed in a man's earliest years, and his patterns were only nightmares.

The nurse came to take the swaddled child from his arms, tutting with disapproval at the doctor who did not know his place. He left and went upstairs to the surgical floor, shaking his head at the nurse who looked up from the desk, her quiet disturbed. 'Don't get up,' he said quickly. 'I'm just going to look in on the MacKenzie boy. No need for you to come.'

Neil was awake, lying in his bed in darkness. Sam leaned against the side of the boy's bed, his hands in his pockets. He had the uncomfortable feeling that he was looking at himself, the younger Sam.

'Can't sleep?'

The boy rolled his head on the pillow, shifted and half sat in the bed. At one time, a nurse must have made the blankets orderly, but now they were tumbled in a wild disarray. Sam shifted himself up on to Neil's bed, sitting with his legs hanging over the side.

'The nurse won't like that,' the boy said with relish. 'She's a dragon lady and she'll kill you.' Neil sat up abruptly, a spasm of pain passing over his face as he jarred the arm in its cast. He jerked his head towards the snoring lump in the next bed. 'He's sleeping because he's got nothing to worry about.'

'You think not?' Sam examined the noisy mound of blankets. 'He's probably got his share, maybe more than you.'

Neil's fingers tortured the blanket lying in chaos across his legs. 'What the hell would you know.' His chest heaved an unsteady breath, his eyes evading Sam. 'You don't have any idea. Doctors are——'

'Fat cats,' suggested Sam easily.

The boy stared intensely at Sam. The doctor's sleeves were rolled up, exposing muscular forearms that hadn't come from putting stitches in wounds. His neck, rising from the open collar of his shirt, looked heavy and strong, too. Above the throat, a granite chin. Neil realised uneasily that if he met this man in the street, wearing grubby clothes, he would turn the other way and run. He decided that the nurse would probably not say anything to Dr Dempsey about sitting on the bed. She wouldn't dare.

'Where'd you get that scar?'

Sam remembered the night he had met Alex. She had half believed that he had got the scar in a street fight. Smiling, he said, 'In the bush. I felled a tree on top of myself.'

'Yeah?' Neil shifted himself restlessly in the bed, protecting his weak arm. 'That was pretty dumb.'

'Yeah, it was.' Sam grinned. 'I'll guarantee I won't do it again.'

'I'll bet!' Neil laughed, his eyes seeming suddenly to sparkle in the dark. 'You learned your lesson quick.'

The man in the next bed shifted in his sleep, the snores abruptly ceasing. Sam said quietly, 'I had a few months lying in hospital to think it over. Hospitals are a good place for thinking.'

'Yeah, I guess.' Neil pushed the blankets away from his legs. 'I bet you never stole a car.'

Sam stared at him for a long moment. Finally, he said slowly, 'You'd be wrong. I was every bit as much of a fool as you.'

Neil licked his lips, his jaw working, his eyes riveted to the man's face. It was half-dark, the light from the corridor mixing with moonlight from outside and bathing the room in an unearthly glow. The doctor's face was even harder than he had thought. Tough. He tried to imagine the doctor stealing cars, and he thought that he could see it, just barely. What he could not believe was that the doctor had been caught. The doctor was a winner, not a loser.

Sam leaned forward, his eyes blackness without form, yet hard and determined for all that. 'If you think I got away with it, that it didn't touch me, you're wrong. Dead wrong. I got caught, just like you. You were joy-riding, right?' The boy nodded, hypnotised. The man said, 'That's what we called it.' Sam's voice grew tense and ironic. 'What the hell, we weren't hurting anyone. Just take a car, have a bit of fun with it, and put it back— well, maybe not exactly where we found it, but they'd get it back. Isn't that how it is, Neil?'

Neil felt his chest constricting. A pulse in his arm pounded painfully. The doctor's voice was low, hardly carrying to the other end of the bed, but it was hard and filled with a suppressed something that Neil didn't want to hear.

Staring down at the boy's shadowed face, Sam realised that he had started something that would change his life more than the relationship between a man and a boy. He was not sure where it would end, but he was involved.

Her mother was immaculately dressed. She swept through the door as Alex opened it, and Alex wondered why she never relaxed, why she never wore jeans or a sloppy shirt. Frances swung around as soon as she was inside, talking in a high voice before Alex could get a word in.

'What do you think you're doing, Mary! Hiding out on a shack on the wharves as if you were some criminal!'

Frances Houseman seemed blind to the luxurious deep-pile carpet she stood on, the beautiful antique furnishings, the walls hung with original oil paintings. She glared at her daughter, and opened her mouth to carry on the tirade.

'Mother, I——'

'I don't understand you.' Frances' voice seemed calm, then abruptly rose to a shriek. 'What got into you? What if people find out? What if——? What about—about Mrs MacAvoy.'

'Maggie, you mean? I don't know what I would have done without Maggie and Michael. I think I'd have gone insane.'

'Does she—does she know——'

Alex thought it was better not to tell her that Maggie was in the kitchen and could probably hear every word. 'Mother, it's not a secret we can keep. I'm having a baby. Sooner or later everyone will know.'

'No!' Her mother's hands gripped each other cruelly, the straps of her bag still hanging from her left arm. 'It needn't—you could—could go away. We could—maybe to your Aunt Lexie for a time. Lord knows, she should feel tolerance for what you've done.'

Alex stood up abruptly and found herself saying what she had often thought, 'Mother, Aunt Lexie is a very—a very warm person.' The adjective seemed to imply a criticism of Frances, and Alex hurried on. 'I don't know what Lexie did to make you feel so critical of her, but I—well, I don't really want to know, and I wish you'd——' She broke off at the expression on her mother's face. This could easily turn into a raving lecture, and Alex felt her courage ebbing. She said hastily, 'In any case, Lexie's off sailing. Don't you remember?'

Her mother seemed not to hear the last comment, which Alex had thrown in as a hopeful distraction. 'Mary Alexandra, we are talking about your situation. This is no time for a misguided defence of your aunt. You are in a mess! We must act quickly to—to preserve your reputation.'

Alex took a ragged breath. How could she have thought she was ready to handle her mother? The woman had the determination of a steam-roller. 'Mother, I—I've thought of going away, too. Of course I have. I've even thought of . . . not having the baby.' She swallowed.

'Perhaps,' her mother said slowly. 'Your father, of course, would have to be convinced. However, I'm sure I could persuade him that it would not be unreasonable in the situation.' She nodded, her eyes glazing over slightly. 'Yes, that would be the best. Then no one need know. You could go to—I suppose to Vancouver, or Seattle or somewhere.'

'Vancouver,' Alex heard herself saying. She gave herself a shake, trying to break the irresistible spell of her mother's will. 'Mother, it isn't going to happen like that. I'm—I'm going to have the baby, and—I'm not giving it up for adoption. I'm going to keep it.'

'You—Mary Alexandra, it's just not possible! You're—you're the daughter of the minister. We have to——'

Alex felt a rigid band of panic and terror tightening around her lungs and heart. 'I—it's my baby, my life.' Her words rushed on. 'I have to—I know it would be—well, embarrassing for you to have a pregnant, unmarried daughter underfoot. So I—I think it would be a good idea if I moved out.' She should have done it years ago.

Why had she come back after university? Why hadn't she struck out on her own then? She loved this woman, but she absolutely must get free to live her own life, away from the inhibitions of being the daughter of the manse.

'You're—what? Move where? You've got to support yourself, you realise, and money doesn't grow on trees.'

'I'm aware of that,' Alex snapped irritably. 'Do you think I'm a fool? I——'

Her mother cut her off with a furious tirade. Alex managed to shut out most of it, catching only a word here and there. She heard Emily Derringer's name, and her father's position with the church. She fought against an inner voice that insisted that everything would be all right if she acceded to her mother's wishes, agreed to be a good girl and do what she was told.

'In any case,' her mother finished dogmatically, 'you can't support yourself, and we can't afford a separate apartment for you, so that's the end of it. The clinic in Vancouver——'

'No! I'll get by.'

'How?' demanded her mother. Alex considered telling her about the book, but decided that that wouldn't help anything.

'Don't worry,' she insisted stubbornly. 'I've got some saved, and I'll get a job.' There was a motion at the doorway to the living-room. Alex looked past her mother and saw Sam's broad form. Maggie must have slipped into the corridor to let him in or perhaps, being Sam, he had simply walked in.

'A job!' her mother shrieked. 'If you could find a job in these times, you'd have found one long ago!'

'Maybe I've been too fussy. I'll find something.'

Sam leaned against the door-jamb, as if he was settling in for as long as it took. Why was he here? Yesterday she had sent him away. Some day they would have to talk again, about the baby, but she had asked him to leave her alone.

'What will you find?' her mother demanded. 'Where will you work? The banks are full, not taking applications. I know that, because Emily told me. And the canneries—you can't work in the canneries with a baby coming. It's hard work, on your feet all day, and the smell of the fish—I can't have my daughter working in the canneries!'

What was Sam thinking, listening to this, Alex being berated by her mother like an infant. He should be laughing, but his eyes on her seemed sombre and perhaps even sympathetic, although he was doing nothing to stop the verbal lashing from her mother. Meeting his eyes, she felt strength flowing into her, a warmth that filled her and made her stand more erect.

'Mother, I'm not a child. I'll make my own decisions on this. I don't know exactly what I'll do, but I'll be the one to make the decisions. Not you!'

'You——' Frances took a deep breath, her hands clutching at her elbows so that she seemed to be hugging herself. Then, swiftly, she turned and saw Sam lounging in the doorway. 'You!' she screamed. She swung back on Alex. 'I suppose you're going to let him keep you! You'll be the scandal of the town, and we'll be shamed! For heaven's sake, Mary! I don't understand you! If you must keep the baby, then marry the man! Make it respectable.'

Her face rigid with anger, Frances swung around with a hard, smooth motion and swept through the doorway, refusing to move to one side to dodge Sam as she went. Sam, equally stubborn, did not move to let her pass. Her suit jacket whipped past him and she was gone with an angry huff and the slamming of the door in the hallway.

Alex put her palms to her face, felt the skin burning.
She would be flaming red, some combination of
embarrassment and anger infusing the flesh throughout
her body. 'I'm sorry, Sam. She—this is hard for her. She
never thought her daughter——' She gulped. It was too
much, too much for her parents and too much for her.
She would shame them. People would be talking in the
pews of the church, passing gossip about the daughter
of the minister as he stood up to give his sermon. Wild.
Just like her brother.

Sam stood immobile for a long moment, watching her,
assessing. At length he said, 'She's not the first parent
to be made distraught by her daughter.'

She whispered, 'My father's the pastor and——'

'They're parents,' said Sam firmly. 'And you are not
a child. You can't live your whole life in their shadow.'
He came further into the room, and said drily, 'She's
right, I did ask you to marry me, and the offer still
stands, of course. It could be the best solution, but I
don't want you accepting just from her pressure. You're
obviously not comfortable with it, and——'

'Sam,' she interrupted gently, smiling wryly, 'you're
not comfortable with it either, are you?' Her eyes
searched his and found the unease she knew would be
there.

He laughed then. 'I've got to admit that, Alex, but—
well——'

She nodded. 'You're offering because it seems like the
right thing to do? I do know about that motivation. I
know—oh, Sam! You've no idea how nice it is to laugh
about something! Everything's so heavy and serious
and—it's terrible, but I really feel that I need some fun
in my life right now.'

'Well——' He pushed back his unruly hair. His smile
made the scar deeper, brought creases to the sides of his

eyes, but his eyes remained serious although warm. 'Will you put yourself in my hands? Put on a jacket and come with me. I have something I want to show you.'

It sounded like heaven, to go with Sam and forget all the heavy pressures. I'd go anywhere with him, she thought suddenly. The knowledge overwhelmed her in a breathtaking flood. 'What is it, Sam? What are you going to show me?' He did not reply and she felt curiosity stirring. 'Won't you tell me?'

As she settled herself into the bucket seat in Sam's Corvette, she remembered how nervous she had been the first time she was in this car. She watched him settling behind the wheel, remembering that she had thought him sinister looking. She had thought he might be a gangster, the scar from a knife fight or some other, nameless violence. Yet she had trusted him, a stranger. She did not know a lot more now, except that he was a doctor, and that he could not walk away from an unborn child he had fathered. She still trusted him, and she was afraid that she loved him, too.

She must not think about that too much. It would show in her eyes and he would see. He would feel guilty if he knew that she loved him, and trapped, because he was the man who could not let himself love. Inconsistent, she thought, thinking of stories she had been hearing. 'I'm hearing rumours about you,' she said, fastening her seatbelt, concentrating on the buckle.

'Oh?' He slipped the car into gear and set it rolling across the gravel and mud car park. 'I haven't killed any patients yet.' He grinned at her suddenly and she found herself smiling back as he added, 'Neither have I been in any street fights.'

She managed to look sceptical and he laughed. She asked curiously, 'Isn't it the time of day that doctors should be in their offices?'

'It is,' he agreed, 'But I got called away early this afternoon to deliver a baby. However, the young lady arrived before I got to the hospital.' His lips curved as he remembered the scene he had found in the delivery-room. 'The nurse was pretty young, and I gather she'd been trying to tell the mother to try to wait, not to push. The mother was an old hand, though, and she wasn't about to wait for anyone, much less the doctor. I got there in time to pronounce everyone healthy.'

'So you didn't go back to the office?' She was fascinated by the open joy in his eyes. Would he feel like this when his child was born? What if she did agree to marry him? Would it grow into love and joy?

'I'm playing hooky,' he told her with a smile. 'I called and all my appointments have been cancelled. Nora Bramley assumed I'd be the rest of the afternoon with the delivery. No emergencies. I guess it's too nice a day for anyone to want to spend it in the doctor's office. So I decided to please myself.'

She felt her heart pounding wildly in her breast and could not meet his eyes. Was this his pleasure, to spend time with her? Did he realise what he had said? She thought not. She pushed the hair back from her face nervously. 'I heard you were in court this morning.' Sam glanced at her, then returned his attention to his driving. 'Did you go in to stand up for Neil MacKenzie?' Sam nodded and she said, 'I'm glad. I've always liked Neil.'

'You know him?'

'About ten years ago I used to baby-sit for him. He was a nice kid—smart. He was always taking things apart—alarm clocks, radios. I was never sure if he knew what he was doing, and I was sometimes worried that he'd electrocute himself. I used to baby-sit for the MacKenzies for a couple of years, then his mother died and everything changed.'

The car stopped for a red light and Sam turned to watch her. 'What happened?'

She frowned, trying to remember details. No one had told her directly what had happened, but she had overheard some things and pieced together others. 'His dad fell apart. I was—I guess I was about seventeen. It was the year I graduated. So Neil must have been about nine or ten. There was a lot of drinking. Neil, I think, was left on his own a lot. Then he got picked up for shoplifting, and somehow that led to Social Services taking him away from his father. He was in the Group Home for a while, then foster homes. I lost track of him.'

The light turned green and Sam eased the car across the intersection and up another hill. Prince Rupert was all hills and valleys pressed between the ocean and the mountain. Sam said, 'As far as I can make out, there were five or six foster homes after that. Probation has the details a bit foggy, and Social Services was vague, except they say the father turned Neil over to them, said he couldn't handle him. He's been in the Group Home these last few weeks, although I guess they haven't seen much of him.' He curled his fingers around the steering wheel. 'Today, in court, they released Neil into my custody. His case will come up for trial in the fall assizes.'

So Neil had a respite, and Sam had taken charge. 'What will happen in the fall?'

Sam parked against a kerb high on the hill. They had passed her father's church and driven on to the very crest of the hill. Between the houses, Alex could see glimpses of the ocean, although her view was blocked by a big old two-storey house with a large glassed-in veranda at the front. Sam turned away from her, and studied the big tree in front of the house. 'That's going to depend on Neil. He's charged with theft and he's guilty. On the other hand, he's young, and he hasn't been in serious trouble before. If he could walk into court in the fall and convince the judge that he's done something constructive with his life, he might manage to get his sentence suspended.'

'What can he do? He's about seventeen, and he didn't finish high school, did he?' Sam shook his head and she said, 'There's a lot of kids around looking for work. Do you think he might go back to school?'

'He can take upgrading at the college.' He had evidently found time to do some research. 'Right now he's still at the Group Home. He'll stay there for a week.' Sam grinned and said, 'Then he comes to me, and I've warned him that he'd better be prepared to work. I plan to keep him busy! From now until fall, he's not going to have time to even think about his old street friends.' Sam got out of the car. She scrambled out of her side and caught up with him on the pavement.

'Sam, why are you doing this for Neil?' He shrugged and she said, 'I'm glad you are. He's got good stuff in him and I hate to think of him wasting his life, going to gaol.' She touched his arm. 'But why, Sam?'

He turned and looked down at her, his eyes shuttered. She met his gaze, and slowly it seemed that she could see through the barriers as he appeared to relax. Finally, he said, 'I don't know, exactly. I guess the kid reminds me of myself at his age. And he needs someone.'

She frowned and said very softly, 'That's a pretty big move for a man who's paranoid about family life.'

'Yeah,' he agreed with a wry laugh. 'And I don't mind telling you that, when I stop to think about it, it scares the hell out of me. But if I've got charge of the boy, I'd better have somewhere to house him. Come on! I want you to look at this place.'

He grabbed her hand and started walking up the pavement towards the house with the large veranda. She found herself being towed along, protesting, 'This place? You—are going to rent it?'

'Buy it.' He had a key out and she could see the 'For Sale' sign on the lawn. She looked again and saw that a big 'Sold' sticker had been placed over the sign.

'You?' She stopped sharply and stared up at the house. Right now she could not see the ocean at all, but there would be a panoramic view from inside. 'Sam, this place is—a house like this isn't very easy to sell if you decide to move. It's so big, and——' She pulled away from him, studying his face with an increasing sense of worry.

He wasn't smiling, although his words were light. 'Last night I called up the real estate agent in the middle of the night and made an offer. He wasn't very pleased to be got out of bed, but I guess he'll forgive me for the sake of a commission. I—what are you laughing about?' He was glaring at her. She had the incredible idea that he felt defensive, embarrassed by his own feelings about the house.

'Sam, do you know whose house this was?'

'Knight,' he said, the name meaning nothing to him. 'It's part of an estate. The owner died last year, and it's been on the market ever since.' He added defensively, 'I got it for a pretty good price.'

'Old Mrs Knight.' Her giggle broke into open laughter. 'Emily Derringer's mother.'

'You're kidding!' He pushed back his hair, his laughter joining hers. 'Damn! The old biddy told me she had a house for sale when she was in the office, but—I never dreamed this was it! On the agreement for sale it was registered to the estate of Mrs Knight.' He pulled on her hand. 'Well, come and see it anyway. Tell me if you think I'm insane.'

As he held the door for her he said, 'I've been staying at the hotel, trying to decide what I want to do. I really don't want an apartment. I—well, I started looking around. Last week I found this place. I wanted it right away, as if—— Well, this is the only place that really appealed to me, although I know it's impossibly big, but I—I just like the place.'

'It feels good,' said Alex, walking past him when he opened the inner door. There was a big staircase sweeping up from the entrance. 'What a banister,' she said with a smile. 'I wonder if Neil's young enough to enjoy sliding down it.'

The stairway divided the lower floor into two sections. She opened a door on the left side and found herself in a large room that had obviously once been a study. She passed through it, and found a big window at the back of the house. There was a large area of grassy lawn back here, ideal for private sunbathing or children playing. The high fence would prevent children from falling down the steep hillside.

She murmured, 'Even Emily must have been happy here as a child.'

She understood why the house had captured his heart. The hardwood floors, the large windows, the antique furnishings that had been sold with the house, all seemed to combine to create a warmth that would make a person feel treasured, comforted. It would be hard to feel stress and tension here.

But it was big, built in the days when the well-off families wanted kitchens and pantries, breakfast-rooms and dining-rooms. Upstairs there were four big bedrooms and a store-room, and downstairs you could have housed a family of four with no problem.

After he took her around the house, she went out to the veranda. This was one of the oldest streets in Prince Rupert. The lots were sizeable and many of the houses were obscured by large old trees. 'You could make this veranda into a lovely area,' she said slowly. 'If it were mine, I'd have my breakfasts out here.'

She turned to look back at him through the open doorway and found him running his fingers over the mahogany of the banister. He saw her watching and said with a smile, 'It reminds me a bit of Jake's place—in Vancouver. He and Jenny bought this big old place. Impractical as hell, I think, but I like the place. Every time I go there for dinner, I find myself wishing it were my house.' He stared at his own fingers as they lovingly caressed the satiny banister, then pulled his hand away self-consciously.

Intrigued, she left the window and moved to his side. 'Sam,' she said softly, touching his arm fleetingly. 'This scares you, doesn't it? The idea of being a home owner.'

'Yeah.' Nervously, he pushed back hair that had not yet fallen out of place. 'Pretty silly, eh?'

She sat on the second step, her chin in her hand, pensively watching the front door. 'I'm not exactly in a position to scoff,' she said wryly. 'As you might have noticed, I have some of my own problems and hang-ups.' He chuckled, then stepped up and sat down beside her. She could feel his thigh pressing against hers.

'I thought of dividing the lower floor,' he told her, gesturing to the study door beside them. 'There's already a door, and it would only need a separating wall in that back hallway to have a self-contained suite with bath. That side door gives a private entrance.'

She nodded, visualising the separation. The left side of the downstairs formed itself easily into a three-room apartment with bath. 'What about a kitchen?'

He frowned, his fingers picking a piece of invisible lint from his slacks. 'I thought of using the old pantry. That would make it complete, and having a suite would make the whole proposition a little more reasonable, not one man rattling around in a massive old barn.'

'Two people. You said Neil would be staying with you? You talked as if——'

'Yes, he will, but he's a young man, Alex. That won't last. I just hope to get him on track, try to let him see he has some choices in his life. He'll be off in a year or so, off to college, or a job. And the apartment, it——' He turned to face her and she realised how terribly close he was sitting. 'Alex, I know you're feeling that you need to be somewhat independent, but——' He gestured vaguely. 'I'd like you to consider coming to live in this house. It's going to take time for the income from that book to come in. If you'd let me give you the apartment to live in——'

For a breathless moment she had thought that he was about to ask her to marry him again. It would have been insane, because he did not love her, but she had been going to say yes. She bent her head and let the dark hair fall into a glossy curtain between them. 'I can look after myself. I will manage. I—I need to be—I really need to prove to myself that I can live on my own.'

He jerked away from her and began to pace the hardwood floor. He looked angry, or frustrated. 'Alex, you could be as independent as you wanted. If you're worried that I—— We could seal off the connecting doorway. It could be just as if you were in an apartment with strangers on the other side of the wall.'

It could never be like that. She would heard the door and know he was close. Even without the sounds of doors and footsteps, she would feel his presence when he was in the same building. His voice was very low, muffled because he was facing away from her. 'It's my baby, too, Alex. You've got to accept that I'm responsible. I guess you're right not to marry me, but I'm—I want to help you support that child, to bring it up. I—— ' He broke off, then the words seemed forced from him. 'I hope you're not going to try to keep me out of the baby's life.'

She shook her head wordlessly. She could never do that. She had seen his face, knew how moved he was by the life he had created.

'You could be free to get on with your writing,' he said. His back was rigid as he studied something on the window-sill. He pushed his hands into his pockets, causing the fabric to strain across his buttocks. 'I work long hours myself, so you wouldn't have to see too much of me.' He turned slowly, confronting her with eyes that were expressionless. 'I could have renovations done to give you a nice office. You'd probably want the study as a bedroom, but I could——'

She shook her head. 'Sam, that old dining-room—it's perfect already. I could put a desk in the window, with bookcases. It would be a beautiful place to work.' She could see herself there. She could work when she felt the need, knowing that no one would call her away. She would not have to hide what she was doing. 'It's tempting, Sam, but—well, if I did accept, my mother would be right, wouldn't she? You'd be keeping me.'

He looked down at her with a frown in his eyes. 'So what, Alex? Don't I have a responsibility to do that?' He grimaced, not liking the sound of his own words, knowing that it wasn't the way to persuade her. He added very gently, 'Alex, I would like you to say yes. I would like to do this for you.'

She was silent for a long moment. The desire to be independent of everyone, to be free, warred with what she felt for this man. And practicality. She had only a little money, and it would take time to get more. If she accepted Sam's offer, she could feel free to devote her time to writing. Otherwise she would need a pay-packet almost at once, and she had no real prospects for a job.

She stood up. He was a patient man, standing almost motionless, watching her, giving her time to think without making her feel pressured. 'What about a compromise,' she suggested hesitantly. 'I'll take the apartment. I'll pay half the going rate for rent, and the utilities.' He frowned and she said quickly, 'Sam, I can't take it for free. You're right, I do need help, but—well, it's got to be a reasonable amount. I mean——'

He nodded wryly. 'You're trying to tell me that you're willing to let me help support the baby, but not you?'

'Yes.' She nodded. 'That's it.'

He walked through the doorway to the study and looked out over the town to the water. He concentrated on a sailboat that was tacking behind a large freighter on the other side of the harbour. 'You drive a hard bargain, Alex. You realise that I'm not used to this. I'm used to getting my own way.'

'I believe it,' she conceded with a laugh. 'You doctors are all the same. Egos the size of houses.'

They laughed together then as he said, 'That's why I picked such a big house, to house my massive ego.' The sound of their laughter echoed into the empty study. 'We'll fix that,' he said. 'I don't know what happened to the furniture in this room, but we'll bring some furniture in here, get rid of the empty sound.'

She looked around at the floors. 'Emily probably took the desk. It must have been a big old desk to fit this room. Sam, do we have a deal?' she asked uneasily, thinking of the furniture and wondering how to approach the issue. She would need a bed and a table at least, but she was not about to let him buy furniture for her. She made her voice businesslike and said, 'Is it agreed? Half the rent, and I pay the utilities?'

'Half the rent,' he agreed easily, adding, 'But I pay the utilities. If we're going to split the electric bill, I'd have to get an electrician in here and rewire the whole place, put in a separate service. It would cost a fortune.'

'Sam——' She faced him, scepticism in her eyes. 'I could give you an allowance for the electricity. Add something to the rent for——' He shook his head and she thought she saw a warning flash in his eyes. It was true that he was used to getting his own way, she thought, and she had pushed him a long way from an insistence that they marry. 'All right,' she agreed abruptly. 'You pay the utility bills.'

'There's just one more thing.' He came close, combing her hair back with his fingers, holding her eyes with his. 'I'm not in any hurry for the money, and it's going to be a while before you have any to spare. Why don't we agree that you pay me the rent when you get your first royalty cheque?'

CHAPTER SIX

ALTHOUGH it was easy enough to laugh about Emily Derringer in Sam's presence, Alex found herself avoiding the woman. There was no reason to believe that she knew about Alex's pregnancy, but Alex knew that Emily would be the first to know when the word got around, and she dreaded the moment of confrontation.

Meanwhile, the secret was safe enough—temporarily. The MacAvoys certainly weren't telling anyone. Alex didn't even know if Maggie had told Michael, but assumed she had. It was hard to imagine Maggie keeping any secrets from the husband she openly adored.

Her mother was not about to spread her shame, and her father never talked about anyone's affairs. But, naturally, on the day Alex moved her things out of the manse and into Sam's recently acquired house, the whole town of Prince Rupert knew.

Sam and Neil helped her to move. It should have been a tense day. Her mother was sternly disapproving. Her father had disappeared for the day. Alex had hardly seen him since returning home from her stay with Maggie on the waterfront. It hurt, realising that he was avoiding her.

It was obvious that in her parents' eyes she was quickly descending the road to hell, yet when she walked out of her old home it was as if a shadow was lifting from her life. Across the street, a neighbour was staring as Sam loaded her boxes into a borrowed truck. Alex saw the curiosity, but it seemed not to matter.

'Why didn't you bring your Corvette?' she teased Sam. Neil laughed as he came up carrying a light box in one hand, balanced with the cast on his other arm.

Sam grinned and shook his head at them both. 'You can ride in the Corvette, but the boxes can't.' They shared the front seat of the truck, Alex riding between Sam and Neil. 'You've grown a bit,' she told the boy.

'Yeah,' Neil said gruffly, almost the first word he had spoken to her. Later they sat in the confusion that was her new home and shared a bucket of Kentucky Fried Chicken. Neil seemed tense, until Alex said, 'I don't know why I brought that radio. It hasn't worked in months.'

'I'll look at it,' offered Neil. He used a kitchen knife to open the case as she and Sam sipped at cans of Coke.

'You don't have a television?' Sam asked her.

'No. I'll write my own stories. I've got lots to do without television.' Her eyes were on the bay window, planning how she would turn it into an office for herself. Neil was sitting there now, her radio in pieces on the seat beside him.

'Don't work too hard on the writing,' Sam cautioned, his hand touching hers fleetingly. 'You need time to relax, too. Look after yourself.'

'Look who's talking! Aren't you the man who works long hours, who says I'll hardly see you although we're sharing the same roof?' She followed his gaze to the window, and said quietly, 'That's the Neil I remember, happiest when he had something in pieces. He's always loved things that plug in or wind up—— You know, you might want to talk to Michael. He's an electronics engineer, and he's planning that big marine centre. He must need employees, and I'm sure Neil has an aptitude for electronics. Maybe——'

'Maybe,' agreed Sam, his voice very low. 'I'll talk to him, but we can't make things too easy for Neil. He's got to work for his own breaks, to realise he's the one who controls his future.'

And from what Alex could see, Sam certainly made sure that Neil worked hard. The doctor was away, as he had predicted, for long hours. He often went out in the evening to the hospital, and sometimes she heard the door at night, followed by the muted roar of the Corvette's engine. Each day, whether he was present or not, he made sure that Neil had plenty to do. First Neil washed down the walls in the upstairs bedrooms, then painted them with fresh, bright paint. Alex was worried about the boy working with only one arm, but Sam ignored the arm and Neil seemed determined to do his work.

Once Alex's belongings were moved into her rooms, Sam left her mostly alone. They shared a kitchen. She heard him coming and going, heard his car, but she saw little of him.

'Don't worry,' he had said that first night. 'I know you want to be independent. I understand that, and I'm not going to be under your feet.'

She had felt irrationally irritated by this pronouncement, but after all she had asked for it, had told him that her independence was important.

She explored her part of the house, including the back hallway that led to the kitchen they shared. Sam hadn't mentioned a dividing wall again since that first evening, and she hoped he would forget the idea entirely. She went down to Safeway and bought a few groceries, then to the telephone store to arrange to have a phone put in. The girl who took her request at the telephone store was brightly curious. She recognised the minister's daughter.

She asked to have the telephone listed under the name Alex Houseman. It felt like a final step, revoking her old identity as Mary. As she wrote out the cheque for the deposit on the telephone, she realised that the money was going quicker than she had expected. Soon her advance for the book would arrive, but until then she would have to be very careful of her few hundred dollars of savings. It was just as well that she had not argued Sam out of his determination to defer payment of her rent. Her mother must be convinced that she was living off Sam, totally dependent on him. Everyone would believe that.

Two Sundays passed. For the first time Alex could remember, she did not go to church. She admitted to herself that she was afraid. Of Emily. Of her mother. She withdrew into her rooms, content to spend her time making them hers. The room that must once have been a children's playroom now held a bed and bureau from one of the upstairs bedrooms.

The second night of her occupancy, Sam brought her an antique desk just the right size for the bay window. 'There's tons of stuff in those upstairs bedrooms, Alex. Go through them and see what you want down here. Neil and I have all we need in those two bedrooms we're using. Anything you want from the others, tell me or Neil and we'll bring it down.'

She shouldn't. Sam was doing too much already.

She concentrated on organising her things, but she badly needed a bookcase for her books. She told herself that she could not start writing until she had the bookcase, but the truth was that she did not feel like writing yet. Soon. One day she would sit down, stare out over the harbour and finish her second book.

The old study became her living-room, outfitted with a sofa and easy chair from a small sitting-room on the other side of the house. 'How many chesterfields can I use?' complained Sam when he moved it in for her. 'You may as well have this one.'

He was strong, used to moving heavy things. She took pleasure in the glimpses she had of him. Sometimes sleek and formal in his suit, dressed for his role of doctor. Sometimes rough and virile, dressed more for a construction site than an office. When he brought the sofa he was wearing an old T-shirt and paint-stained blue jeans, his muscles so hard and prominent through the thin cotton that she had to clench her hand to keep from reaching out, touching, caressing.

Her dreams of him were spreading, moving into the daylight hours. Perhaps it was the new hormones in her bloodstream. Did pregnancy make a woman more sensual?

She enjoyed making her breakfasts in the big old kitchen, taking a small tray with her and sitting in the big chair in her living-room, looking out with the window open. Soon she would start working. She felt as if she had her own world here, as if no one could intrude from outside.

Finally the day came when she wanted to work. She would go upstairs and look for a bookcase, then she would do some work whether she found a place for her books or not. She could hear Neil upstairs, and she found him in an empty bedroom, with furniture pushed out into the hallway. He was standing on a chair painting the walls with a roller.

'Are you sure you should do that with your arm in a cast?' she asked, worried, seeing more the young child he had been than this half-man.

'Of course,' he scoffed, grinning at her. 'If it wasn't OK, Sam wouldn't ask me to do it. I've already done the next room.'

She went and looked, then came back and told him, 'It looks nice. You're doing a good job.' He glowed with the praise and she wondered how often anyone had taken time to give him a kind word, a moment of caring.

'After this,' he told her, 'Sam wants me to clear out the basement. Then I'm to get to the yard. There's a motor mower, but it's not working and I'm supposed to fix it.'

She frowned. 'Do you know anything about mowers?'

'I'll figure it out.' He was determined, and she thought that he would do anything Sam asked.

She watched for a while, then asked, 'There's a small bookcase out in the hallway. Are you or Sam using it?'

'Nope. You want it? I'll bring it down for you after I finish this wall.' He was working steadily, using his injured arm for balance. She hoped he would not fall from the chair.

'I'll carry it.' She was probably fitter than he was.

'No!' He swung around sharply, teetering on the chair. 'Sam says I'm not to let you lift anything!' He glared at her a little nervously, then said tensely, 'You gotta let me carry it! Sam would be mad if you did it.'

Sam didn't want her to lift things because of the baby. Neil didn't know about the baby, or she thought he didn't, but Sam had given instructions. The bookcase was small, but Neil was determined and Alex was shaken to realise that Sam was thinking of her even when he wasn't around her. 'All right,' she agreed finally. Neil heaved a sigh of relief. How had Sam got such a hold on this boy?

Neil brought the bookcase down, carrying it balanced with his one good arm and his shoulder. Luckily it was small, although she shuddered as she heard him coming down the stairs. It would be terrible if he fell and hurt the arm again because of her. He put it in place beside the desk, then stood looking around, saying, 'This is pretty nice.' He was tall and terribly thin, towering over her but looking as if a stiff wind would blow him over. 'You should have some rugs, though. There are some upstairs. I'll get them.'

He was gone before she could protest, returning three times with braided scatter rugs that seemed to tie her furnishing together with the polished hardwood floors into a bright warmth.

'Thanks, Neil. The colours are perfect.' He was smiling, sweating slightly, his breath still coming rapidly from all the trips up and down stairs. She asked, 'What do you do for lunch?'

'Grab something.' He shrugged. 'Sandwich or something.'

'Have lunch with me,' she invited.

It became a routine for them. In the weeks that passed, she saw more of Neil than she did of Sam. She worked on her book in the mornings, had lunch with Neil, then in the afternoon she took a walk by herself before working again at the computer.

The new book was unfolding as if it had already been written somewhere in her subconscious. She was still doing her newspaper articles, too. She had gone down to the newspaper office and talked to the editor, with the result that she was now doing two articles a week instead of one. Two evenings a week for the articles. Her days for the book. She wrote a letter to her literary agent to give her new address and the telephone number for the silent phone that had been installed.

Neil started afternoon classes at the college. 'Upgrading,' he explained as he ate his omelette one noon hour. 'Then I might be able to take the electronics technician course. The instructor says I don't need much more to qualify for that. Mostly some maths. And I'm good at maths.' To take the electronics course he would have to stay out of gaol, too. She didn't say it, but Neil frowned and she thought he was thinking of his next court date.

She learned little things about Sam from Neil, although Sam seemed so busy that even Neil saw little of him. Enough, though, to keep him busy. 'He knows how to make a guy work!' Neil complained one morning as he sanded the banister. His voice sounded proud, as if it were an honour to have the doctor as a slave-driver.

In the nights she listened when Sam went out. He often did, returning an hour later, perhaps two. For the most part Sam was keeping his promise to leave her alone.

One day her mother telephoned. 'There's mail here for you,' she said abruptly. 'I'll leave it on the kitchen counter.'

'Mother——' But she had hung up, and when Alex went to the manse she found the house empty, a long envelope lying on the counter. She had been avoiding her mother, nervous of seeing her, but the empty manse wounded her, making her feel like a traitor. Had she done the unforgivable, by sharing a time of wonder and joy with Sam? What they had shared had been so complete, so beautiful, it was no wonder that a child had been created in those hours they had spent together. How could anything so beautiful be wrong?

She took the envelope home. It was from her agent.

'Here you are, Alex Diamond. Publisher's advance on *Holy Murder* enclosed, less my agency commission. Publication date for hard-cover edition is February 1.'

Her book would go to press just a couple of weeks before the baby was due. She wanted to tell someone, but Neil was at the college, and Sam of course was at the clinic. She paced, hugging her excitement to herself. She finally sat down at her desk, but she couldn't think about work. The cheque in her bag was for something she had written. *Her book* was going to be in print, perhaps even sold in the downtown bookshop.

Emily was a mystery buff. Perhaps she would be buying Alex Diamond's book. Alex turned the computer off, having typed not a word. She had to tell someone about the cheque. She picked up the telephone and dialled Maggie's number, but there was no answer.

The person she really wanted to tell was Sam. She opened the telephone book and looked up the number of the medical clinic, but she hadn't the nerve to dial and talk to the receptionist who might recognise her voice.

She grabbed a light jacket and went outside. She decided to walk downtown rather than take her scooter. The bicycle had a flat tyre and she hadn't got around to asking Neil to fix it. She had nothing to do all afternoon except put the cheque in the bank, and it was a beautifully sunny summer day, perfect for a walk.

The teller at the bank was bright-eyed with curiosity when she handled Alex's deposit, and she would have asked a question if her supervisor hadn't been standing close by, watching.

How long would it take her mother to hear that she had put a large sum of money into the bank? Alex went to the Safeway and bought three of the most expensive steaks she could find. Mushrooms. Tomatoes. She filled a basket with enough for a lovely steak and salad dinner for three. Neil had said that Sam loved pumpkin pie, so she stopped at the bakery and bought a pie. She had never been in a liquor store in her life, and she found herself very uncomfortable as she walked along the aisles and tried to decide what would be a nice wine for dinner. In the end she bought a half-case of beer, because she remembered Sam saying over a table in a Vancouver nightclub that he was more comfortable with a bottle of beer than a glass of wine. The assistant stared at her oddly when she asked for a bag for the beer, but she knew what kind of talk would be going around town if anyone saw her walking along the street with an armful of beer.

She was paranoid, always thinking about what people were saying. She knew she should stop it, but it was too deeply ingrained, too much a part of her life.

She found walking up the hill to be hard work on her way home. She was out of breath and far too warm by the time she let herself into the house. Usually she went directly to her own part of the house, avoiding intruding on Sam's privacy. Today, for the first time, she succumbed to the temptation to walk through Sam's side of the house to the back hallway.

He kept his living-room very tidy, although a few magazines scattered around showed that he spent time here. A medical journal. A computer magazine. A regional magazine from California. Sam was from the United States originally. Where? California? It seemed insane that she did not know.

Beside his chair there was a book of poems by Rudyard Kipling and a science fiction novel that she had been meaning to read ever since she saw it on the stands a month ago. There was a very good stereo on an antique table. She remembered the table from her first visit here, but the stereo was new. Sam's. There was little else she could see in these rooms that had not been there when he had bought the house.

He had so few things of his own. It was as if he only spent money on the things that were very important to him, but then he spared no expense. The quality stereo. The car. The impossibly big house. Neil.

And his unborn child.

She had to swallow the tears, and there was no reason for crying. Except that he was a man who should have a lot of love, and he had spent most of his life alone. She knew that he would never tell her all the details, but she was piecing them together from the things she knew, and the things she picked up from Neil. He had been dragged from one home to another all through his childhood, had been beaten and screamed at and everything but loved. It was a wonder that he had emerged from his rough upbringing still able to give. He had gone out on a limb for Neil, had offered Alex far more than she could accept on behalf of their child.

Yet he asked for nothing. Neil was working hard for Sam, but Alex knew that Sam was not making him work for any reason other than the boy's rehabilitation. He was doing the same thing with Alex. He had bought the house, given her this apartment, would give anything more if she asked—except himself. But the only thing he had accepted from her was the gift of her innocence, and that only because he had thought he would never see her again.

She stood in the kitchen, staring at the steaks on the counter, realising that she would have to be the one to change that. Somehow, she must make him aware that he could reach out to her without danger. That wasn't going to be easy, especially for someone as shy as she was. Shy? she questioned, impatient with herself. She was a coward, a raving, rabid coward!

The first step was the telephone, terrifying though it was. She had the number memorised. She doubted if she would ever forget it.

Mrs Bramley's voice was brightly efficient. 'I'd like to speak to Dr Dempsey, please.' Alex was proud of the businesslike tones she managed.

'The doctor's with a patient. If you'd like to leave a name and number, he'll get back to you later.'

A name. Of course. You never called a doctor and got straight through. 'Alex,' she said, feeling panicked. 'Just ask him to call Alex, please.'

'Alex? Do—isn't this Mary Houseman?'

Alex took a deep breath, wishing herself far away from this telephone and Mrs Bramley. She said stiffly, 'I'm calling myself Alex now.' And that sounded so insane that she added defensively, 'It's my second name.'

'I *thought* I recognised your voice. All right, Mary, I'll tell him. You did say Dr Dempsey? Not Dr Box? Did you want an appointment?'

'No!' Her heart was thundering and she had to escape this. She said hurriedly, 'Thank you. I've got to go,' and she got the telephone receiver back in its place. She shouldn't have done it. He would be furious at her calling his office, disturbing his work. He'd said that he worked long hours, and that was just a polite way of telling her that he was not to be disturbed. He had made it sound as if she was the one who would not be disturbed, but he was the doctor and everyone knew you didn't barge in on a doctor's day unless you could show blood haemorrhaging, or a bone sticking out through the skin.

You certainly didn't call because you wanted him to come home to dinner. They would all be talking about it, and Sam would be angry because his staff would be gossiping and speculating behind his back. Did Mrs Bramley know where Alex was living now? Alex stared at the telephone for a long time, then managed to convince herself that she was a fool to wait for his call. She hadn't left a telephone number and, although Sam was probably aware that she had a telephone installed, he had never asked for the number.

She tried to get back to work on the book. Chapter six was finished, and she had the words 'Chapter Seven' staring at her from the monitor. In chapter seven the murderer was going to discover that the girl who lived in the barge alone was actually Mr Awley's daughter, and she had all that in her notes. It seemed dry and dull. She couldn't think of one interesting way to start the scene and it seemed to her that no one reading the book would care who the girl's father was.

Someone knocked on the door. The front door. Sam's door. She was incapable of ignoring a knock, even if it was probably not for her. She left the computer turned on, went through her doorway and into Sam's hallway. She hesitated, but the knock was repeated. She pulled the door open.

He was wearing his cleric's collar, but he looked uncomfortable in it. At first he said nothing and she had no words either, except, 'Daddy,' as if she were still a small child.

He pushed his hands into the pockets of his suit jacket. 'Mary, can I come in?'

She stepped back, wordlessly. He followed and turned as if to go into Sam's living-room. 'No,' she said then. 'This way.'

She opened the door and he followed her, his eyes taking it all in, but his lips silent. She led him to the easy chair by the window. 'I'll get you a cup of tea, shall I?' He usually liked tea in the late afternoon.

'Yes,' he said slowly, still looking, not ready to meet her eyes. 'That would be very nice.'

He had no idea what to say to her, and she was no better. They sipped tea together and finally he said, 'Mary, is everything all right?'

'Yes.' She sipped on her tea and avoided his eyes.

'Do—ah, do you need any money? I could——'

'No!' She steadied her cup before the tea spilled. 'I'll be all right. I—I've got some saved, and I've—there's a good prospect of a job.'

Her eyes went to the computer. She opened her lips to tell him, but the words would not come. He would think that Sam was keeping her. Everyone would think that. It would be better, far better to tell him about the books. She wasn't sure why she didn't. She almost called him back when he was going, to tell him. Her lips were open, but then he turned and said, 'I'd like to see you in church,' and she felt an unreasoning anger at him because he had not once asked about the baby, as if he could pretend that it did not exist.

Duty, she thought. He had come because he felt he should. Did he really want her in his church? Embarrassing him? She felt confused and uncertain, warring with the urge to run after her father and try to explain everything to him.

Would he ever understand about Sam? He did not understand his sister, her Aunt Lexie, because Lexie was impulsive and a bit wild. Yet sometimes she thought that he had understood the wild spirit in Toby. What did that mean? Wild. For Toby it had meant drinking and drugs, but what had Lexie actually ever done that was so terrible? This year she had answered a personals ad and had gone sailing with a man she hadn't met before. That might be foolish, but Alex could not believe that it was evil or wrong. Mother had very recently announced that Mary was taking after her aunt.

Opening her arms to a stranger on the beach.

She walked slowly into the kitchen, staring at the steaks. She still hadn't decided whether to put them into the freezer for another day when the noise shattered the quiet around her. It was the first time her telephone had ever rung since the day it was installed. She dashed to it, jerking the receiver up and gasping, 'Yes?'

'Alex? Are you all right?'

She felt the breath hissing out of her, like an empty balloon. Sam, and she didn't know what to say. 'Yes, I'm OK. I—I just—I'm sorry I bothered you at work.' She ran her free hand along her thigh, smoothing the denim jeans that were never meant to be smooth.

'I'm not bothered.' Amazingly, he laughed. 'I needed a break. I've just been listening to the trials and tribulations of a sixty-year-old woman who has wanted to leave her husband for thirty years.'

'Oh.' She giggled. She had a crazy feeling that she probably knew who that woman was. 'Do you tell everyone about your patients?'

'Only you.' He was smiling. She could close her eyes and see it, the scar a deep line among the other lines of laughter and sorrow. 'It's terribly unethical, but I know that you're good at keeping secrets.'

'I am,' she agreed, and the sun came out from behind its cloud and turned her living-room into a brilliant happiness. 'I got a letter from my agent.'

The doctor holding the receiver on the other end found himself on the verge of saying that he had a soft spot for the literary agent. If Alex hadn't made that trip to Vancouver to meet with the agent, Sam would never have met her. He closed his fingers hard on the receiver, told himself not to be a fool, not to stick his neck out, not to talk without thinking first. 'What did she say?'

'That the advance came, and she was enclosing a cheque, and the book is being published in February.'

'That's great news.' He could hear her joy and it brightened his office. 'You've got to let me read that book one day. Are you coming out of the closet in February? Are you going to tell people?'

She was silent and he wished he'd not spoken, but she had to face it some day. Finally she said, 'I don't know. I called—I wondered if you'd like to—could I make dinner for you and Neil tonight? Sort of a celebration?'

'I'll take you out instead,' he decided impulsively. 'It's your victory. You shouldn't have to cook for it.' He and Neil usually went to McDonalds, but tonight they would go somewhere special.

'I'd—I'd like to make dinner for you.'

'All right.' He closed his eyes and tried to remember what had been on the appointment book for him this afternoon. 'Whatever you want. I can't get home until about six. Is that all right?'

'Yes. It's fine. Sam? I'm sorry I called the office.'

'Why? Call any time you like.'

He heard the distress in her voice and didn't understand it at first. 'I—I said it was Alex, but Mrs Bramley recognised my voice, and—they must know where I'm living, the people at the clinic. They know me, and—they'll think I'm living with you. They'll be talking and—Sam, I'm sorry.'

Impatiently, he said, 'Alex, why should it be any big deal if they think we're living together? It's not—for heaven's sake, Alex! Dr Halchuck is living with Dr Waddelsey's wife—ex-wife, I mean—and has been for years.'

'I know that, but we're not. We're—I'm——'

He sighed. 'Does it matter, Alex?'

'People will think——'

His nurse tapped lightly on his door and he said in exasperation, 'Honey, in a few months they'll damned well know!'

'Maybe I shouldn't be living here. I——' Alex broke off and shivered uncontrollably. She didn't want to leave.

She wanted to be here, close to him. Her lips said, 'Sam, if I'm living here they'll think it's your baby.'

'It *is* my baby, and I should damned well hope that everyone will know who the father is! You can forget the idea of keeping any secrets about this, Alex, because everyone is damned well going to *know* exactly who the father of that child is! It's my baby, too, and I'm not staying out of its life to keep another one of your damned secrets!'

Her fingers were white on the receiver. 'I'm sorry,' she whispered and he snorted in exasperation. 'I shouldn't have called.' He said nothing and she knew how angry he must be. She whispered, 'Goodbye.'

'No!' The word echoed and she waited, not knowing what she should say. She hated arguing with him. Finally he said softly, 'Does this mean I'm not invited to dinner?'

'I——' She laughed shakily. 'Oh, Sam, of course not!'

'I'm not invited?' he teased.

'You *are*!'

He could still hear her voice in his ear when he replaced the receiver on its cradle. He stared at the chart in front of him, but it was Alex in front of his eyes.

They would have supper together tonight. Sometimes in the last few weeks he had heard her moving around in the kitchen they shared, and he had made himself stay away, give her the room she had said she needed. Tonight he would not stay away. He would watch her as she prepared the meal. When she came to the table and sat down across from him, he would pretend that she belonged to him, that they were together, facing the world as one.

She was his woman. She had belonged to him ever since he had found her, a pirate's wench on the beaches of Vancouver.

I love her. Those words kept coming back to him, but this time he acknowledged them, wishing her voice back in his ear. He felt a powerful surge of need overwhelming him. His hand trembled on the cover of the chart, crushing the light cardboard. He wanted desperately to feel her smooth skin under his fingers, to possess her; yet the need to see open love in her eyes was greater than his powerful drive for possession.

He knew that there was fear mixed equally with his need, his love, but there would be no more running. He had a long way to go, he realised, his fingers smoothing the next patient's crumpled notes. Jake and Quade would laugh. He had fallen in love with a woman who had more hang-ups than he had.

It might be easier somewhere else, away from all the symbols of her childhood—her parents, the gossip. On the beaches of Vancouver she had been free and loving, reaching out. He did not know if he could do the reaching, touching her when she was holding herself tightly closed. Yes, it would have been easier somewhere else, but he had to use what he had. That meant wooing Alex in the middle of all the people who would try to keep his woman as a child.

He practised the words carefully in his mind, but he wasn't sure what she would say in return. He was terribly afraid that she would turn away, and he knew it might be a long time before he could actually say it to her. I love you.

CHAPTER SEVEN

THE soft sounds of a Strauss waltz drifted in from the next room. Sam leaned back in the dining-room chair, lifting his glass to his lips. Alex watched his throat move as he swallowed the cool liquid. He looked very relaxed, content. He had shed his jacket and tie. She could see the base of his throat where a few dark hairs curled through the open neck of his shirt.

A few moments ago, Neil had finished his dinner and gone out to the theatre with a new friend from his class at the college. Until then the conversation had flowed easily, but now Alex felt tense, casting about desperately for something to say. Sam had seemed undisturbed by the silence between them. A few moments ago he had gone into the next room to put on some music, then returned to relax with his beer.

'I should do the dishes.' Alex stood up and started stacking plates.

'I'll help,' he offered, although he sounded disgruntled.

'It's all right. I don't need any help.' She balanced the salad bowl on top of the plates, added the cutlery along the side, and at the last minute picked up a bottle of salad dressing in her right hand. She turned to go into the kitchen, keeping her eyes on the pile and walking slowly.

'Careful,' cautioned a husky, low voice right behind her. Startled, she swung and found Sam only a few inches away, one hand outstretched as if to help balance the

precarious pile of dishes and salad. 'Watch out!
You'll——'

It was too late. A fork fell and she jerked back,
throwing the whole mess off balance. The salad bowl
was leaning at an impossible angle. She reached
desperately for it with her right hand, forgetting the
dressing. She felt it—heard it go just a second too late.
Then everything went, flying out of her hands. The glass
bottle filled with dressing hit the doorway and seemed
to explode. The salad bowl took off, spinning like a
Frisbee, hitting the wall and sending wet lettuce and
tomato everywhere. A spoon struck one pool of orange
dressing and splashed oily liquid back on to them.

'Oh, no!' She had one plate in her hand. Everywhere
else was wreckage, broken dishes and salad. She started
to step forward and was stopped, a hard hand jerking
her back.

'Watch out!' Sam was almost shouting, gripping her
arm painfully. 'Don't walk into that! You'll get cut.'

'I've got shoes on,' she said automatically. The mess
was everywhere. 'The carpet,' she whispered, horrified.
The orange salad dressing contrasted hideously with the
warm rust and amber tones of the carpet in the dining-
room. She lifted her hand to push her hair back, and
found the plate still hanging from her fingers. As she
watched, a scrap of tomato that had been clinging to
the plate dropped on to the floor by her feet. 'Oh, damn!'

She couldn't even look at Sam. Why was she such a
clumsy, terrible fool? She had meant this to be a wonderful evening, to try to show him what he was missing,
that—well, at least that he might want to spend some
time with the woman who lived under his roof. Oh, hell!
She could feel the tears coming and that was just all she
needed to top it off! Standing here crying like an idiot

while he watched, silent and so damned masculine and attractive, seeing her make a fool of herself.

Her arm was released. The flesh tingled where his fingers had gripped. She stared at the mess, afraid to see what was in his eyes. She wouldn't blame him if he walked out. She would probably not see him again for weeks now, just glimpses of the back of his white car, the sound of the door at night as he went out.

Firm fingers took the plate from her. With both hands free, she combed her hair back into a wild chaos, staring at part of a leaf of lettuce stuck to the elegant wallpaper beside the doorway. 'I'll clean it up,' she mumbled, knowing that the orange spattered on the wall would never disappear entirely until the wall was repapered.

'Hey, Alex——'

She swallowed a lump and pulled away from the kindness in his voice. He must think she was an idiot, a child, with the tears spilling over. Big hands gripped her shoulders, pulling her back against a hard wall that was Sam. His fingers gentle, massaging. His head lowered, his lips against the hair near her ear. She closed her eyes and sagged against him, feeling his broad chest taking her weight easily.

'I'm sorry,' she gulped. 'It was so stupid. I should have carried less and——'

'Stop apologising,' he whispered. 'It's only a——'

'A mess!'

Her eyes wanted to close, to enjoy his touch, but she could see the broken dishes, the gory orange salad dressing, the symphony of raw vegetables stuck everywhere.

'Hey,' he whispered, his hands rubbing down along her arms. She was wearing a short-sleeved dress and his fingers quickly slipped on to her bare skin, making her tremble through the tears. 'It's not all bad. I was hoping for something like this.'

'What?' She spun around, staring at him, forgetting that the tears had run down her cheeks, that she was almost as much of a mess as the damned floor! 'That's crazy! What do you mean?'

His hands guided her closer. His lips brushed a feather kiss against hers. 'I was hoping for a chance to put my arms around you again.' His eyes were deep, dark brown, and they were the whole world. As she stared up, mesmerised, his husky voice whispered, 'And to kiss you again.'

It would have been impossible for her to keep her lips closed against his. He kissed her gently, the warm flesh of his mouth holding hers, then drifting to caress the softness of her cheek, the fluttering dampness of her eyelids.

'Sam——' It was a whisper, hardly a protest, and he paid no heed, his lips returning to cover hers. He felt the lightest stirring of her body against his and he brought her closer, his arms moulding her softness to his hard maleness.

The sun slipped behind the mountain on the other side of the harbour, bending light and sending red streaking across the harbour, bathing their entwined forms in a gentle rosy glow. Alex's fingers explored the coolness of Sam's throat, felt the tremble that spread through his muscular frame as her lips opened to his kiss and he plundered the sweetness of her mouth. Her fingers slipped into his crisp brown hair, clenching as she felt a wave of exquisite dizziness.

His large hands seemed to span her waist, his thumbs caressing the trembling that was her midriff, his fingers pressing into her back. The tightness was spreading all though her chest, causing her breath to come in ragged inhalations. She could feel her swollen breasts touching, pressing against her bra, her abdomen quivering with a growing heat.

When his thumbs moved to the bottom of her ribcage, she gasped, her mind leaping ahead to the caress of his fingers on her breasts. She sagged against him and he shifted to take her weight, his thigh pressing against hers, his tongue exploring the shuddering underside of her lower lip.

She had hungered for this closeness so long, body and soul both starved for his touch, the soft gasp in the back of his throat as she pressed close, her soft curves crushed against the hardness that was his chest.

'Alex,' he groaned, his hands dropping to her hips, holding the firmness of her buttocks as he drew her close, hard against his need. 'I've wanted this so long, such a damned long time.' His head bent lower, his mouth seeking, his shadow sheltering her from the light of the sunset outside.

She had felt it, too, all the nights, all the hours since she first gave herself to this man's hard, gentle hands. Her eyes closed and the world was gone, his arms secure at her back and under her knees, lifting, carrying her. She pressed her face against the hollow of his shoulder, feeling the movement of his muscles under her cheek. Her right arm circled up around his neck and she felt the tension of his corded muscles as he carried her. With her eyes closed she caressed the fine hairs that escaped the open top of his shirt. Under her seeking fingers, his flesh jerked rigidly. She felt an answering pull deep within herself.

Then she was sinking into a dense softness. She opened her eyes and saw the brocade quilt of her own bed. His face shut out everything else. She could see only the harsh lines of him. His mouth was straight, without the slightest trace of a smile. His eyes were molten black, staring down at her as if she was the fate that had imprisoned him. A dark flame burned in the darkness of his eyes, like anger or bitterness. She closed her eyes against it, against the sight of herself relected in his face.

He could see everything, through the fantasies and the dreams, right into the core of her, the trembling and the fear that was the real Alex, the real Mary. 'Don't,' she whispered, and his fingers touched her lips, silencing. Her eyelids opened and found his face smooth, his eyes doused to a deep warmth.

'Don't touch?' he asked, whispering, his fingers trailing across her throat, brushing towards the swelling of her breast.

The pinkness of her tongue slipped out to wet lips that were suddenly dry. She shook her head, her throat too parched for sounds to escape. His lips came to hers and she felt all the inhibitions melting away, her arms reaching up to pull his head closer, her lips opening and her tongue meeting his, mouth opening eagerly to his invasion.

He was lying beside her, slipping one arm under, his other hand sliding the zipper down along her back, sending a long, delicious shiver along her spine. She felt the thin fabric of the dress sliding from her shoulder, his lips dragging away from hers, moving to caress the warmth of her throat, the trembling swelling that disappeared under the lacy fabric of her bra.

'I keep dreaming of this,' he said hoarsely, fingers brushing against the lacy fabric almost as if he was nervous of touching, taking possession.

'I've dreamed of you,' she confessed, and the words were easy to say while his eyes were obsessed with the sight of her.

'I want you to remember.' His thumb hooked under the strap of her bra and slipped it down over her shoulder. Her breast grew full, the edge of lace still covering the swollen peak. His voice was ragged. 'I'm going to be in all your dreams.'

His head bent and she could see only his hair, the curve of a suntanned ear. She felt lips touch the bare flesh at the same time that the warmth of his mouth penetrated through the thin fabric. His teeth gripped the edge of the lace and slowly drew it down, freeing the warm swelling. Cool air touched her engorged nipple. She saw his throat move as he swallowed. His lips parted and he took the hard peak into his mouth, tongue moving softly against her rigid arousal.

Her head arched back, pressing into the pillow, her fingers clenching in his hair. His hand caressed her midriff as lips and tongue explored the warm softness of her breasts. She was going to explode, the heat and the need pulsing through her, head spinning, his touch fire and sweetness, unbearable pleasure, her ears ringing from the passions pulsing through her arteries.

His mouth moved to the underside of her breast, pressing, exploring. His fingers caressed the thrust of her hip as she twisted to her side in a desperate need for closeness. She craved his touch on her skin, not masked by the thickness of frothy fabric, diluted and diffused by distance. He swept the barrier of her skirt aside, his fingertips finding the firmness of her leg, the heated flesh of her inner thigh. All her life she had been waiting for this man, this touch. Her knee bent, legs parting, inviting his caress with a depth of need that she could not have concealed to save her life.

The ringing grew in intensity, louder, repeating, penetrating. She rolled her head in protest, but his fingers stilled and there was only the sound, penetrating again and again from the other side of the house. She swallowed, her eyes opening, her lips moving against the nakedness of his chest.

'Your telephone. Sam——'

She must somehow have undone the buttons of his shirt. She didn't remember making the motions, but his shirt was open to the waist, pushed back, his hard naked heat pressed against her. The last echoes of the sun were almost gone, the room thrown into black and white, Sam's face strangely white against the darkness of his hair. His eyes closed and she felt a shudder go through his entire body. She could feel the immediacy of his need, their bodies closely entwined. His fingers drew away from her thigh, across the bunched fabric that had been a smoothly pressed dress.

'I'll be right back. Don't go anywhere.' His voice was hoarse, his lips seeming full and swollen as they brushed hers. 'I have to go. It might be the hospital.'

Her whole body was a heartbeat, flesh pulsing with each surge of life through her veins. She watched as he walked away, towards the door of the bedroom. His shirt was still open and half pulled out of his slacks. It was her impatient hands that had pushed it aside. She closed her eyes when he was gone, trying to breathe steadily, to still the pulsing that shook her lips and her feet, and the molten centre of her womanhood.

Awareness came slowly, sensations flooding past the all-encompassing desire. Her fingers were moving on the roughness of the quilt, caressing as if she touched the man still. Her hands clenched. The room was almost dark now, the furniture standing out harshly against a sky turned grey. She became aware of the paleness of her exposed flesh. She sat up too quickly, felt a wave a dizziness. Her clothes were twisted, the dress a hopeless mass of wrinkles. She adjusted her bra and tried to make the dress look like a decent covering.

His voice carried through the open bedroom door, low and confident, holding none of the tremor that hers would if she were forced to speak. She pulled open a bureau drawer and grabbed at the first thing she found. It was desperately essential to cover herself, to erase the image that was reflected back at her from the mirror.

Anyone who looked would see that she was a woman interrupted on the edge of fulfilment, all soft need and swollen passion. Jeans were better, zipped up securely and feeling a little tight. A shapeless sweat-shirt over the jeans. She pushed the dress into the drawer, sliding it shut with a bang. It would be a patient on the telephone, or the hospital. He would have to go in any case, and it would be better this way. She could not bear for him to return and find her lying on that bed, waiting, looking like...

She jerked the quilt smooth as a board creaked. He was moving, coming back. She swallowed and rushed out of the bedroom, closing the door behind her and leaning against it. Why had she let this happen? He would think that she was in his house because...because she loved him.

He did not want to be loved.

He came through her doorway, stopped when he saw her. For a moment something flashed in his eyes, then was gone. His shirt still hung open, the skin dark between the two pale panels of cotton. He looked tanned, as if he spent long days in the sun, but she remembered the muscled entirety of his naked body and knew that the darkness was everywhere, even on the protected vulnerability of his lower abdomen.

He wanted her. He had said that, but it did not show in his eyes now. They were still, as his face was. The lines were deep beside his mouth, around his eyes, but there was no warmth or need, only a waiting as his gaze took in Alex standing with her body pressed hard against the closed door of her bedroom.

The need was purely physical, she realised. His body had yearned for hers, but now it was gone and she was glad she had covered herself and got away from the bed. She felt a brief yearning of regret, the knowledge that her need was greater, that she would spend a long, barren night.

'I——' He was waiting for her to explain, and she supposed she was doing the unforgivable, going beyond the verge of surrender, then withdrawing. 'Sam...'

She wished he would do up his shirt, or say something.

'I can't, Sam! I just can't do——' She blinked and pushed her hair back. It was a wild tangle. There had been no time to brush it into smooth order. Tonight she would be terribly conscious of him sleeping upstairs. She would want to walk along the hallway and up the stairs to his room. She must not do that. 'The only way— Sam, I can't live here if—— Everyone is going to think that we—I can't stay unless, no matter what the other people think, I *know* it's innocent.'

'Innocent?' He seemed to shudder. 'Alex, just what do you think we're doing? Do you think we're sinning by making love?'

She shook her head mutely, but the noise was rising in her mind, some kind of raucous symphony comprised of other voices. Dad's, quiet and worried. Mother's, high and accusing. Emily's, a smugly knowledgeable whisper. And Sam's, but he was silent now, turning to leave.

'Sam,' she whispered, but he was gone. She waited for the sound of the door slamming, the muted roar of his car starting, but heard nothing. After long seconds she managed to walk slowly across the room, her feet feeling as if she were wading through thick water. She closed the door, shutting him out although he was not there.

She heard the faint sounds of music. So he was not going out. The telephone call had not summoned him to the hospital. No, of course not. He had come from the telephone directly back to her. He had expected that she would be waiting for him, her arms open and eager.

She paced through her rooms, from the closed door to the back where windows looked out on the harbour. She could hear sounds through the hallway at the back. She had closed the front door to her apartment and they were separate, two distinct living areas, but joined at the back. There was no doorway to seal him off at the back, just the corridor that led to the kitchen, then on into his dining-room.

And the mess. The sounds she heard were kitchen sounds. Water running. Dishes clattering. She should go to help him. He was cleaning up the mess. She stood, staring at the corridor, hearing him, hugging herself although the sweat-shirt was more than warm enough for a summer night.

She went into her bedroom, but the sound of water running penetrated even as she brushed her hair hard and vigorously. Standing in the dark, listening to him, was harder than facing him. She stopped at the desk, telling herself that it was the evening for her to work on the newspaper article, but it was a joke to pretend that she could do it tonight.

In the end she was drawn, as if by a magnet. He was not in the kitchen, but the sink held a pile of dishes and the door below swung open, scraps of broken plate sticking out of the dustbin.

He was in the dining-room, scrubbing at the wall with a wet cloth. 'It won't come off with that,' she said dully.

He stopped, his hand still, not looking at her. 'What, then?' he asked, as if there were no other issues between them.

'Maybe some Spic 'n Span,' she suggested, bending over to pick up a shard of glass that caught the light from the overhead fixture.

She took the glass to the kitchen and ran a bucket of water with the cleanser in it. Then she went back and worked on getting the mess out of the carpet while he washed the wall. They hardly talked at all, but it seemed that the tension had eased between them by the time they had finished cleaning.

The next day he called her late in the morning, his voice casual over the phone lines. 'Hi, Alex.' She could hear other sounds around him.

'Sam,' she breathed, sinking down on to the edge of the chair. He was the only person who had called her so far. 'Where are you? I hear noises.'

'The hospital. I've just finished my rounds. I—how about dinner tonight? My treat, this time.'

'You're going to cook for me?'

'Not this time. I thought we could go out. I remember you saying you liked Greek food. There's a Greek restaurant down on third that I've heard is quite good.' He chuckled, said, 'I'm sure you'll enjoy it more than a Sam-cooked meal. That way, I won't risk that I'll throw the dishes all over.'

She giggled, remembering the hour they had spent scrubbing up her mess after last night's meal, although it had not seemed at all funny at the time. 'Do you think it'll be safer that way?'

'Probably.' She could hear warmth in his voice and she smiled although he could not see.

'What about Neil? Is he invited too?'

He paused, then said, 'Neil, too, of course,' and she was disappointed although she echoed, 'Of course.'

'How's the writing going?' The sounds around him were busy, but he seemed in no hurry to hang up.

'Pretty good today. Another body just turned up, so that's two murders.' She coiled the telephone cord around her finger absently, said, 'No one knows who the murderer is yet, of course.'

'But you do?' Someone called his name in the background. He said hurriedly, 'Just a sec, Alex.'

She heard a muffled conversation, then his voice saying, 'Sorry, I've got to go. Is dinner on?'

'Yes.' She would wear something different this time. A trouser-suit, perhaps, something less alluring than the dress from last night. Neil would be there, and there would be no kisses.

CHAPTER EIGHT

NEIL'S instructor at the college claimed that he had finished the mathematics upgrading in record time. Sam and Alex both had reason to know how hard he had worked. He was seldom seen without a maths text in hand as July swept away into August, and he often spent the lunches and suppers they shared talking about factoring equations or solving geometry problems.

The three of them ate together most evenings, Alex preferring to cook for them when she could, because she felt uncomfortable dining in public. She was wearing looser clothes now, and she was afraid that people would look at her and know her condition.

She had still not been to the church, and she had not seen her father again. She glimpsed her mother once when she was shopping downtown, but ducked around a corner and avoided the contact. She knew she was being a coward, but told herself she was being considerate of her mother, protecting her from the embarrassment of meeting her daughter.

One day she caught Neil's eyes watching her as she carried their lunch soup to the table. He blurted, 'You're going to have a baby, aren't you?' and she wanted to run, but she could not let herself.

'Yes.' She put down the soup in front of him.

He was silent a long time, blowing on a spoonful of the soup that was too hot to eat. 'Is it Sam's?' he asked finally.

Would everyone know that? Sam had said he would make sure there was no doubt whose child it was. She closed her eyes, afraid of the criticism she might see in the youth's eyes.

'Yes, Neil. It's Sam's baby.'

It was one thing to theorise about this and to tell herself she could be a single mother, but quite another to have her body growing larger, her secret announced to the world, and herself feeling the terror of it all.

She should go away, somewhere where no one knew her.

She hardly went out of the house at all, except for the dinners with Sam and Neil. She hadn't the nerve to tell Sam of her fears. He seemed to have no sensitivity at all to other people's gossip and she was sure that he would not understand. She would have liked to eat all her meals at home, but Sam insisted on taking her and Neil out two or three times each week. She spent their restaurant dinners with one eye on the entrance, her eyes dropping to her plate when she recognised a customer.

Neil became fussily protective of her, as if she were a fragile treasure. She saw a lot of Neil, because he seldom went out, and when Neil and Sam decided to have a chess tournament although neither of them played, it was Alex who volunteered to teach them in the evenings.

She enjoyed those evenings. At first she helped them both with their moves on the big antique chess table in Sam's living-room. 'If I've got the board, I may as well learn to play,' Sam had murmured one evening, and Neil was eager to try anything that interested Sam.

As they became more skilful, she brought in things to do as she watched them. She got up her nerve to go into a wool shop one day and started working on a big white shawl for the baby. She was embarrassed at first, knitting what was obviously a baby shawl with Sam sitting there, looking over at her from time to time. Then she met his eyes and thought she saw a warm contentment there. He liked seeing her prepare for the child.

Some evenings they hardly talked. Others were lively with conversation. When Alex tried to decide how to commit the third murder in her new book, both Neil and Sam made enthusiastic suggestions.

'Slip a syringe of air into his IV,' advised Sam.

Alex shook her head. 'Can't. He's not in the hospital. He's healthy as a horse—a very obnoxious man. Just the kind who never gets sick.'

Sam moved his knight on the board and grinned. 'I think you're bloodthirsty at heart. You want to kill off the poor man.'

'What about electrocuting him?' suggested Neil.

'Sure, I'm willing.' Alex put aside the knitting. She was sitting cross-legged on the carpet. 'Sam, you put Neil in check when you moved that knight.'

'Did I? Oh, yeah. Check, Neil.'

Neil groaned and Alex smiled as she picked up the knitting needles and pulled some of the fine wool free. 'How do I electrocute him, Neil? He's not the type to play with the insides of his own television.'

'You could rig up his car.' He moved his king out of Sam's way temporarily. 'We could get some wire and try rigging up Sam's Corvette. I'm not sure what you could get out of one of those batteries if you built a circuit for it, but they've got a high amperage rating. You might kill somebody.'

'Not the Corvette!' Sam swiftly moved to close in on Neil's king again. 'Guard your queen. And check. Mate, too, I think—and if you touch my Corvette, Alex will have a real murder for her book!'

She had never realised how much pleasure there could be in sharing her fantasy stories with other people who were creative and fun-loving. There was a lot of laughter on those evenings, and her book seemed to be writing itself, once she decided to do her murder with poison and picked Sam's brains for details on poisons a person might be able to buy in a town this size.

Sam watched her whenever he was near, and he watched what she ate. About once a week he reminded her that she should go in for a check-up with Roy Box at the clinic. She always agreed, but she hadn't made the appointment yet. She was putting off the clinic, telling herself that she had a doctor watching her every move, her diet and her complexion. There was no urgency about going to Dr Box. Sam would say soon enough if he thought she was not looking after his child.

Even when he was not in the house she could feel his presence, as if he was thinking of her while he was away. She knew it was the child she carried that he was really caring about, but she couldn't stop herself from enjoying his attention. He telephoned every morning as he finished his hospital rounds. Oddly, those telephone conversations had a flavour more intimate than the meals they shared. In each other's presence they both seemed to shield behind Neil, talking to him more than to each other.

'You should eat breakfasts,' she told Sam during one of their telephone conversations. Every morning she listened to him, heard the shower, then his footsteps running down the stairs, the sound of the kettle as he made himself a cup of instant coffee.

'Can't face cooking that early in the morning,' he told her. 'Coffee is what I really need when I get up.'

'I could cook breakfasts for you,' she offered.

There was silence as she clenched the receiver, regretting her offer because he did not want it. Finally he said, 'Alex, you've no need to do things for me.'

She wanted to. A button had come off his shirt the day before. She had offered to sew it on for him, but he had shrugged a refusal. She didn't know what he had done with the shirt, but she suspected it was pushed into the bottom of his wardrobe.

She did not cook breakfasts for him. She listened instead, and when he was gone from the house each morning she cooked for herself and Neil. Neil went to the hospital one day and his cast came off. His arm was very white and weak, but he was going to physiotherapy three times a week and Sam was pleased with the X-rays of the arm. On Sam's suggestion, Neil had gone down to talk to Michael MacAvoy at the site of his new building. He came back with his eyes bright and excited.

'I've got a job!' he announced to Alex. 'Well, sort of. I'm helping on the building two hours a day, kind of a gofer for Mr MacAvoy. Then, if I do good in the electronics, I might have a chance of a job when my course is over.'

In mid-August he signed up to start the electronics course at the beginning of September. He paid his fees with money he had earned himself. While he waited for the course to start, he spent his evenings reading an electronics book he had borrowed from Michael. Alex hoped he would be able to finish the course. His court case would come two weeks after school started. They had no way of knowing if Neil would be free, or in gaol, after that.

'Try not to worry too much about it,' she overheard Sam telling him one day. 'You're doing everything you can to influence the decision. The schooling, the possibility of a job—it's all going to create a favourable impression on the judge. If I were you I'd go in and have a talk or two with the probation officer before the court date, too. Make sure he knows what you're doing, that you're straight. Then try to put it at the back of your mind, knowing you've done everything you could.'

She knew that Sam had spent some time with the probation officer on Neil's behalf, and she suspected that he had arranged the job with Michael, although he gave no hint of it to Neil himself.

One day Sam came home with a dog, a big Saint Bernard that squeezed its way through the doorway. Alex heard the door and the scrabbling of dog, accompanied by a low 'Woof'. She left her computer and came dashing through her doorway and into the foyer.

'What—where on earth did that come from?'

The big canine head tipped awkwardly to one side, then the feet ambled over to her. A long tail swept across, creating a draught she could feel through her slacks. Her hand automatically dropped to the dog's neck, her fingers scratching the heavy folds of skin and dog hair.

'One of my patients,' explained Sam, looking faintly embarrassed. 'An elderly fellow up at the Manor. He's been worried about his dog, and I told him I'd look after it.' He rubbed the back of his neck, complained, 'I thought I had. A neighbour offered to take him, but it fell through. Apparently he eats too much.'

She smothered a giggle. 'I don't wonder.' She thought of the contents of the kitchen, and said, 'We don't have any dog food. There's the remains of the roast from last night, though.' Ten dollars a kilogram seemed like a high price for dog meat, but Sam wanted the dog looked after so she said, 'He can have what's left of the roast, and I'll get some dog food for him this afternoon.'

'Thanks, honey.' He smiled wryly, and said, 'I really hadn't bargained on this, although he does seem like a nice dog.'

She froze as his hand covered hers, giving the dog an affectionate scratch before his fingers curled around hers. She asked, 'What's his name?'

'Maxwell.'

'Maxwell?' She eyed the dog doubtfully. He was big and awkward, the tail sweeping dangerously. He rubbed his head against her leg, almost pushing her over. 'Max,' she decided. 'I'll call him Max. Do you think the fence in the back yard will contain him?'

'I hope so! I'll go and take a look before I go back.'

It turned out that the fence was high enough and solid enough—at least, Sam hoped so. Alex fed the dog and turned him loose, then walked with Sam back towards his car.

'We'll take him for a walk this evening,' said Sam. 'But don't take him out yourself. Not yet. When I had him on the leash, he was determined to go back to his old home. He's so damned heavy, he really pulls. I don't want you to try to handle him yourself on the lead.'

'All right.' She had no desire to be dragged across Prince Rupert, towed by a big Saint Bernard. She supposed that she should resent Sam's giving her instructions like this, almost bossing her around, but it made her feel warm and sheltered.

Sam stepped out of the way for a bulky middle-aged woman passing on the pavement. The woman stared at Alex as she passed, her rigidly sprayed hair a smooth criticism as she pointedly glanced from Alex to Sam, but said nothing. Sam didn't notice, but Alex did, and she wanted to shrivel. Emily Derringer's best friend, and if Emily wasn't gossiping yet, she soon would be.

Sam stepped closer, frowning. 'Alex——'

She didn't know why he broke off, or what he was about to say. The woman's head was stiff, her ears obviously trying to catch their conversation. Alex felt a sudden, sharp anger. 'Hello, Mrs Santon.' The woman didn't seem to hear, didn't turn, so she raised her voice. 'Good morning, Mrs Santon!'

She jerked, mumbled, 'Oh, hello, Mary. Yes, I—good morning. Ah—how are you?'

'I'm fine.' Why, this woman was as nervous as she was. Alex's voice softened and she said, 'Thank you for asking.'

Helen Santon smiled nervously and scurried down the pavement away from them. Sam's fingers grasped her arm, demanding her attention.

'Alex, when are you going in to see Roy for a check-up?'

'I——' She smoothed her palms on her thighs nervously. Sam's hand didn't leave her arm and he wouldn't look away from her. 'I feel fine.' Her voice was defensive. 'I'm fine. There's no hurry.'

'I should have made you go before this.' He glanced after the woman who had got a half-block away by this time. 'I don't like what's happening to you right now. You're hiding from everyone, as if you're ashamed to be seen. That woman who just passed—she's the first person I've seen you talk to except for Neil and I, and the MacAvoys.'

She pulled away from his hand, but his eyes held her although she wanted to turn and escape into the house. 'They all know me, Sam.' She bit her lip. 'All my life they've treated me—well, differently than other people. In school, whenever the other kids were doing things, everyone assumed that I wouldn't be part of the—well, the fun or the wildness. They talked differently around me, treated me as if I was different. They're all watching now, and they're thinking——' She shrugged helplessly, swallowed her frustration, realising that there was no way he could understand.

'They're thinking you might be human after all.' He gestured after the disappearing woman. 'Of course they're watching you. You've lived an unnatural life. Living in a manse is unnatural for a child. I'd imagine that the average clergyman's child breaks out around the age of seventeen, getting far away from the restrictions. They're watching, quite understandably hoping for signs that you're as human as the rest of us.'

She shuddered. 'They're getting signs, aren't they?' She was living in the same house as an unmarried man, unchaperoned except for Neil's presence. She was losing the figure that had been hers, thickening and filling out in places that didn't come from overeating. 'They'll have all the evidence they can handle.'

Sam exclaimed impatiently, 'Grow up, Alex! That woman down there—don't you think she's got some sort of human weakness in her family? Even your damned Emily Derringer, for goodness' sake!'

'No, not Emily.' She knew that. Emily would never understand, and Emily would spread all the dirt she could. Emily had been whispering, hovering, when Toby died. Alex had always got on well with Emily herself, but she had heard the bite of her gossip and dreaded being the brunt of it herself.

'Alex, you—damn it, Alex! We've got to——' He pushed an impatient hand through his hair, and loosened his tie absently. 'You've got to get over this somehow, but right now you've got to get in to see Roy. Hell, Alex, you're expecting a baby. There are tests that should be done, and——'

'I will,' she promised hurriedly, wanting this conversation over.

'You've told me that before. When?' he demanded. His hand attacked his hair again. 'Look, this has got to be done, Alex. I've let it go too long. I could get Roy to come here, to see you at home, but damn it! You can't hide forever. And the tests have to be done at the hospital, in the lab.'

'Do——' She gulped. 'Are you trying to tell me that you think something's wrong?'

'No!' He shook his head angrily. 'Do you think I'd have let you go this long if——' His voice softened abruptly, lost its angry heat. 'Don't worry, honey. I'm sure everything's fine, but—look, think about it yourself. I know you've had some dizziness, some nausea. That's natural enough, but you should have your iron count checked. You might need more vitamin supplements than what I've brought you. You should have——'

'Sam——' She touched his arm, hurt by the concern in his eyes, longing to be the brave person he wanted her to be. 'I can't face going into the clinic. I can't—I thought I could do this, but I can't—Sam, I really can't do it!'

He froze, deathly still. 'Honey, what—what is it you're trying to say? You—you're not thinking of an abortion? Not now, Alex, it—it's too late— It wouldn't be safe now, and—Alex, it's almost—— There might be a doctor willing to do it, but it wouldn't be——'

'No!' She shook her head vigorously. 'No, Sam. No! I—I wouldn't do that. It's my baby. Your baby, too. I wouldn't—— '

'Then what are you telling me?'

She stepped back, feeling him too close, nervous suddenly of the large strength he radiated. 'I think I should go somewhere else. It would be better if I went somewhere else. I——' She rubbed the back of her hand over her eyes, wishing he wouldn't look like that, his face so shuttered and still. 'Sam, I can't do it here, not with everyone——'

'Alex, people are not monsters.' He sounded very tired. She thought of all the night calls, wondered if he was sleeping well enough. 'You're making this into something it isn't. Of course some people will gossip, but you can be pretty sure that they're the same people who were scorning you behind your back when you were being Miss Goody Twoshoes up at the manse.'

'No——' She shook her head vigorously.

'Yes, darling. The people who matter, the ones who are your friends, like Maggie and Michael—those people don't change. You can run away if you like. I know I can't stop you—damn it, honey, I'll even help you if you really must go. But it's the wrong thing. You don't know——'

His pager beeper sounded loudly, overriding his voice. He closed his eyes painfully. 'You have no idea,' he said harshly. 'You have no idea what you're throwing away if you run now. You have a family here, people who love you. Don't throw that away. You'll—Alex, this is something I do know about. Being alone. You were never made to be rootless, alone, without—— Don't run away from the people who care about you.'

'My family don't——'

His fingers touched her lips, silencing her. 'Give them a chance, honey. You've thrown them quite a curve. Just give them a chance to recover. I have to go now, but—just promise me you won't do anything until we can talk more about this?'

She didn't have to promise, because he couldn't wait for her words. She watched the car roaring away, felt the tears welling up in her eyes. She went inside, where no one could see her if she cried. Through the window at her desk she could see the dog, Max, rolling on the grass, trying to scratch some elusive spot in his thick coat. He seemed content and she wondered how long it would be before he started to whimper, crying for his old home, for the old man who had been his master.

She sat down, mechanically rereading the words she had typed on the screen earlier. This was a dramatic scene, filled with suspicions and fear and the developing sensual attraction between the heroine and the man who might be the murderer... He wasn't, but the heroine had no reason to know that yet.

Her fingers moved. New words streamed across the screen, but they were stilted and wrong. She frowned, pushing her hair back behind her ears and then forcing her fingers to type, making the words keep coming. Two sentences. Three. A paragraph.

Her hands stopped. Outside, the dog raised his head and stared intently. On the other side of the fence a Siamese cat was stalking a bird, preparing to pounce. Max's tail moved, sweeping the grass as he watched the cat. His thick, heavy body froze, on the verge of motion, then he dropped back into a blob on the lawn as if involvement was too much effort.

The doorbell rang. Alex started to rise, then sat down again. It was the first time in her life that she had ever ignored a telephone ringing or a doorbell, but there was no one she wanted to see. She read the words on the screen. She had typed a line of gibberish as she watched the dog. She highlighted it to delete, then found her fingers continuing the highlight, erasing everything she had just written.

There was no future for her here. Hiding from the town, waiting for Sam to come home... watching for Sam... talking to Sam on the telephone... always wanting more. If she invited him, he would take her body to his, making love to her, and her need would quickly grow into an obsession.

But he would accept nothing from her except the physical act of love. He shoved his shirts into the wardrobe rather than ask her to sew on a button, refused to let her give him breakfasts, paid for a meal for her for every one of his she cooked.

He was never going to let himself need her, except in a physical way. She closed her eyes, shutting out the bright day. She could feel the vulnerability growing inside herself. The tears were close. That happened so often lately, the desire to throw herself down and sob wildly. She supposed it was partly hormones and the baby growing inside her, but it wouldn't be long before she would be begging him, reaching out and asking for anything he would give her.

She had a terrible conviction that he would give anything she asked—except himself. The more he gave, the more she would need. Then she would be possessed, belonging totally to a man who needed no one, who had learned to stand alone as a child.

She knew where she could go, knew how she could escape all of this. It had come to her out there on the pavement as Sam had pressed his demand for her to go for her check-up with Dr Box. She could go to Aunt Lexie's house. Her aunt was away sailing, but her small house on the outskirts of Victoria was empty. In her letter, Lexie had said that she was not renting the house, but leaving it in the care of the next-door neighbour.

Alex knew the neighbour, and she was known in turn. If Lexie were home she would welcome her niece in her casual fashion, telling her to push something aside and make a place for herself. As it was, the neighbour would let her in and Lexie would not mind when she found out.

Oh, lord! She was going to miss Sam terribly. The other day she had thought that there was something, some movement within her womb. She had been playing

a game of chess with Sam in his living-room, and she
had almost told him, asked him to touch and feel what
might have been the first stirrings of their child.

His son, Sam had said once. She hoped it was a boy,
if that was what Sam wanted. If she stayed here any
longer, she would be reaching out, clinging, asking him
if he was still willing to marry her. He would say yes,
but it would be a trap for him. She knew a lot about
this man. He would never walk away from anyone who
needed him. But he needed no one. Except sometimes,
in his eyes . . . but he never reached for her.

She should be working, writing, but she knew that she
would do nothing more today. Perhaps there would be
no more words written under this roof. Sam would say
she was a coward, running, hiding, and it was true. She
had faced one dragon today, forcing her to say hello
because of a surge of uncharacteristic anger that she
didn't understand. If Sam loved her, needed her, she
thought that she could stand tall and face them all. It
would not matter.

He had needed her the night he had made love to her
under the trees. That was what had made it right, and
it was why it had been so inevitably easy to give herself
to him, to ask him to take her. But that night was gone
into fantasy, never to return.

I love you, she thought, watching the dog he had taken
in. She knew she would never be able to say the words.
She would have to content herself with loving his child.
He would always be in her life, through the child, but
he would not belong to her or to anyone. She had been
pretending that, shutting herself away here as if it were
their world and he were hers. It wasn't true. He belonged
to anyone who needed him, his patients and Neil as much
as her. It would never be different.

She got out her bank book and a piece of paper. She had to telephone BC Ferries to check the fares before she could calculate what she would need, but she had enough, just enough to get her to Victoria and last until the baby came. Her book was being published then, and she was due the second half of her advance on publication date. She could make it if she cashed in the savings bonds that had been her graduation present from her parents. Thank heaven for the medical insurance which would cover the costs of her delivery!

Sam would insist that she have her medical check-up before she left, and she should do that. She telephoned and made the appointment for the next day, ignoring Mrs Bramley's curiosity. It didn't matter. The ferry left in two days, and she would be gone. They could all talk as much as they wanted then.

He had said he would help her if she felt she had to leave. She would not need his help, just the knowledge that he would not stop her. She looked at her watch, but there was no need to make a lunch for Neil today. He was working mornings on Michael's building site, afternoons at the college. He had packed a lunch to eat at the college before his classes. She would eat soon herself, because she had to look after herself, but there was no hurry.

She walked slowly around her own rooms. There wasn't that much to pack. A couple of suitcases, and she would ask Neil if he could crate up her books. Perhaps Sam would not mind storing the crate in the basement for a few months. She wouldn't be able to stay at Lexie's forever, but later there would be more money. There was no reason to think that her next book would not sell. She herself believed that it was better than the first.

She went to the kitchen and poured herself a glass of milk, taking it with her up the broad stairway. She set it down on the bedside table in the bedroom that was Sam's. The shirt was where she had thought it would be, stuffed into the wardrobe. The button was in the pocket. Sam was a surgeon and if he could sew up people he could probably sew on a button. It didn't matter. She wanted to do it, although he would probably never notice.

Then, when the shirt was mended, she would wash it with her things in the washing machine down in the basement. Once that was done, she should start packing. There was not very much to pack, but it would be best to have it done, while the numbness inside her persisted.

The next two days were not going to be easy. She would have to hold herself against the feelings. Thankfully, tonight was the night Maggie had invited them all to supper. There would be fast talk and laughter, and she need not say many words to Sam.

Tomorrow would be a business day. She would arrange things, and she would have to tell Sam she was leaving. She would postpone that as long as she could, avoiding being alone with him.

Her parents would have to know she was leaving, but, cowardly or not, she could not face them yet. She would write a letter and post it on her way to the ferry. It would be easier for all of them that way. No awkward contact.

CHAPTER NINE

HE KNEW that Alex had made some decision.

Through most of the dinner at the MacAvoys she was silent, as if content to listen to the conversation. But it was in her eyes, the gaze that would not meet his. He watched the thick dark lashes fanning over her cheeks as she stared down at her dinner plate.

Maggie was animated, telling them about the fireworks that had ensued today when a fisherman had moored his fifty-foot boat outside a twenty-foot speedboat. Young Dixie was heatedly arguing the chess game she had lost to Neil, a dispute that seemed to show that neither of them had the rules very clear in their minds. Michael was laughing, his usually cool grey eyes sparkling at Maggie. 'Listen to that wife of mine! Another war on the wharves! And you're the lady to keep them all in line, darling!'

'Well, he's not going to do it again!' said Maggie heatedly, and Sam believed it. He wouldn't have wanted to be on the wrong side of Maggie himself, and he suspected that she and Michael had their share of battles although they obviously loved each other very deeply.

As Maggie told the tale, Alex's interest had been caught and she had come out of her pensive stillness to give Maggie a half-smile. 'Which one of them won't do it again? The fisherman or the speedboater?'

'Both of them! The pleasure-boater knew better than to moor in an area reserved for commercial fishermen! But the fisherman—that stupid turkey Solly! He's such a hothead.' Sam almost laughed alound, because if anyone was a hothead it was Maggie MacAvoy. She added, 'I had to kick Solly out last fall, and I should never have let him back!'

Michael leaned across and combed Maggie's wild curls back, his eyes warm. 'Alex, some day you should get her to tell you about the wars between Solly and Rex. The first time I saw Maggie, she was standing between the two of them, all five foot four of her facing down two big, angry fishermen who were trying to kill each other over a dog!'

Sam saw Alex's dark eyes sparkle. 'You know,' she said slowly, 'it's a wonder there hasn't been murder done down here. Think of it!' He recognised that look in her eyes. Her mind was busy putting together the tendrils of a plot. 'The night I came here, Maggie—remember how dark it was?' Maggie shook her head, but Alex said, 'Pitch-black. It was low tide and the lights were shining so high above the wharves that there was no light down where I was walking. Lonely. Dark shadows of boats stretching across the planks.' She absently chewed on a forkful of salmon, and mused, 'I think I'll murder someone down here some day.'

Michael jerked, startled, and Sam assured him, 'She's not really violent. She does all her murders in fiction.' Then he smiled at Alex, but she had gone away from him again.

Her eyes were glazed over with a pensive worry, the dusting of freckles across her nose emphasising the paleness of her skin. Her hand was guiding the fork in an aimless abuse of her salad. It wasn't like her at all. She always had a healthy appetite, and she laughed easily. Her eyes should be glittering, because she loved listening to Maggie's waterfront stories. He restrained an urge to cover her restless hand with his.

She was going to leave him. He had never had any claim on her. In Vancouver, it was as if she had walked into his life and wrapped her fingers around his heart, terrifying and charming him at one and the same time. She had felt it, too. Damn it, he would swear there had been love in her eyes then—when she was a mystery lady with no last name.

He wanted to give her all the things that he had never had himself. A home. Love. His arms around her when she was afraid. He wanted to help her. He *could* help her if she would let him. He had spent half an hour with her father last week, campaigning for him to say a good word for Neil in court this month. The Reverend Oliver Houseman had been helpful, courteous. As they parted he had asked gruffly after his daughter. Sam had searched his eyes and asked softly, 'Why don't you come and see for yourself?'

Given half a chance, the pastor would reach out to his daughter. The mother would be harder. In fact, she would probably disapprove forever unless Alex agreed to marry him. He had trouble believing that Alex and her cool, efficient mother had ever been truly close.

The thing was to approach her parents together. First ask them over to dinner, let them see that their daughter was happy and content, that—well, let them see that Sam loved her.

Damn! Why was it impossible for him to go to her parents and tell them plainly that he loved Mary Alexandra Houseman—Alex Diamond—whoever she was! Hell! She had said it would be better if she left, and she had decided now. She was nervous of telling him, but it was in her eyes.

He was terrified that both she and the unborn child would slip out of his life forever, as so many other people had done all through the past. He had almost asked her in the car earlier. They had stopped on the way to the MacAvoys' to have a look at the newly erected walls to Michael's building. Michael had been there, just leaving for home, and Neil had elected to go on to the docks with Michael because he wanted to ask him some questions about the reading he had done.

Sam had driven the rest of the way in silence, alone with Alex, trying to work out words to ask her not to go. He had parked at the Rushbrooke car park, the wheel still gripped between his hands, his mind forming words his lips would not pass.

Damn it! He was afraid. He was thirty-eight years old and he hadn't let himself care if anyone walked out on him or kicked him out for over twenty years. Now he was terrified that if he asked her, and she said she was going, he would be begging her to stay. He must not do that! It was no good, clinging to people.

His beeper went before the dinner was finished. Not now, he thought desperately. He had arranged with Roy to cover his calls tonight. He needed every minute with her, tonight especially, while there might still be some chance to change her mind.

'I'll phone in and check,' said Sam.

Perhaps it would be quick and easy, and he would not have to go out. He had to be here to take Alex and Neil home. He was almost certain that she would go walking alone with him if he asked her once they got home, in the seconds before she disappeared into her rooms. Then, alone with her on the empty streets...

'Dr Dempsey? Thank goodness we caught you! It's Mrs Mallory.' The voice of the emergency-room nurse was briskly efficient. 'The ambulance brought her in on an MVA. Dr Box is attending. She's haemorrhaging badly. He's ordered her prepped for an emergency C-section. Dr Box wants to know if you can operate.'

He glanced at his watch, said, 'I'll be there in ten minutes—no, five.' Thankfully, he had turned down the wine before dinner. He had needed a clear head for Alex, and now he would need steady hands. Why hadn't Roy called in the gynaecologist? No, the man was away at a conference, and in a city of this size there were no back-up specialists. He pushed aside a memory of Celia Mallory's last visit to the office.

'Here's your jacket.' He hadn't realised that Alex had followed him from the dining-room. Her eyes worried, her hand touching his with fleeting warmth as he took the jacket and slung it over his shoulder.

'I'm sorry——' he began, but she shook her head.

'Don't, Sam. Michael can give us a ride home.' She smiled, walking with him to the door as if she understood that he could not stop even for these few words. Her fingers grasped his arm as he pulled the door open. 'But drive carefully. You can't help anyone by getting killed breaking all the speed records between here and the hospital.'

He nodded. 'It's a car accident. A——' There was no time. Her lips were parted slightly as she looked up at him and he let himself have the indulgence of one quick, hard kiss. As if he had the right to promise her everything with his lips. 'There've been enough accidents tonight. I'll be careful.'

The sweet honey of her lips was with him as he drove. He kept to the speed limit, because she was right and he would only save thirty seconds or so by speeding. Celia Mallory needed him in one piece tonight.

Although he had prepared himself for it to be bad, he was shocked when he saw her. His eyes met Roy's above the masks and for a moment he wished for the anonymity of a big hospital. He remembered clearly the last time he had seen this young woman. 'Four weeks,' she had said, laughing, touching the swelling lovingly. She already had two small children and a husband she loved. Both the previous pregnancies had been without incident, the deliveries uneventful. She had wailed, 'Dr Dempsey, I'm not sure if I can wait four more weeks. Are you sure this isn't twins?'

He'd laughed, enjoying her pleasure. 'Not twins. You saw the results of the ultrasound.'

'Who have we got for the baby?' he asked Roy now. The baby would be born under anaesthetic and might have sustained injuries in the accident.

'I called Alan in.' Roy adjusted the drip on the intravenous tube that led into the woman's arm.

'Good.' He was glad to see Wendy step up beside the instrument tray. They were all good. Wendy and Alan and Roy, and he knew that his own steady hands were skilful, but tonight they would need more than skill. He breathed deeply, calming himself, praying that they would be able to save Celia and her baby.

Alex tried to sleep, and she succeeded after a time, but she was awake the second the car drove up, alarmed without knowing why. Her eyes came open and she listened, hearing the low sound of his engine. She waited for the slight rev that he always gave before he turned the engine off. She did not hear it, nor did she hear the car door slamming, his footsteps on the stairs.

It was too long. Something was wrong, terribly wrong. She got up, feeling her way in the dark, belting her dressing-gown over the white frothy nightgown as she hurried to the door, not stopping to find slippers to cover her bare feet.

Yes, it was his car out there in the shadows, the white catching what little light there was from the street-light across the street. The engine was still running, although quietly. She couldn't hear it until she was outside, halfway along the pavement to where he was parked on the street. But she could see his silhouette. His head was leaned back against the head-rest.

'Sam?' The driver's window was partly open. His face looked as it had the night she had first met him on the beach.

'Sam?' She opened the door, shifting her feet on the cold pavement. He didn't look at her. 'Sam, are you all right?' He nodded finally, his eyes still closed. She crouched down to see him better, positioned herself so that he had to see her too if he opened his eyes. 'Sam, what is it?'

He shook his head slowly, his hands still on the wheel. She took the hands in hers, turned them and stared down at his palms. They were inert. She curled his fingers around hers.

'Nothing, honey,' he mumbled. 'I'm all right.'

She knew that it was not true. He should not be alone with the hurt she could see shut inside him right now. 'Come with me into the kitchen. I'm going to get you some tea.' She pulled on his hands, but he was too heavy. If he didn't help there was no way she could get him out of the car.

'Don't bother,' he said then, his voice low and toneless. 'I'll just go up to bed.'

'No!' That got through. His eyes focused on her and she said sharply, 'Sam, come on! Come into the house!' She reached across and turned the key off, then pulled his arm to urge him out of the car. He came docilely and that was so uncharacteristic that it worried her. She closed the door behind him and led him into the kitchen, pushing him down into a chair at the table.

He sat there silently as she moved around, plugging the kettle in, getting out the teapot. He acted as if he was in shock, but she was no doctor. She had never even taken a first-aid course, although that seemed like a criminal oversight right now. She didn't know if tea was right. It seemed to her that the remedy was something hot with lots of sugar in it, but Sam hated sweet tea and coffee.

The main thing was to get him moving, get him talking, somehow snap him out of this. She put the steaming cup on the table in front of him and was relieved to see him pick it up. She pulled out the chair next to him and sat down, watching him intently and with determination. 'Now, Sam, tell me what happened.'

He was closed, shutting it all in. She watched him drink his tea, and hoped the warmth would help somehow. 'Thank you,' he said dully as he put the empty cup down. He stood up. 'I'm going up to bed now,' he said, his mind not on his words, or on her. She knew that he was still back there at the hospital.

His feet were very slow on the stairs, taking him up under automatic pilot, she supposed. There was a floor-board in his room that creaked, but it only sounded once. She hugged herself, standing alone in the kitchen in her bare feet, hating the thought of him alone up there.

She rinsed their cups, then went outside to close the window of his car and lock it. She did it mechanically, knowing that she had to go to him. She was nervous, a little afraid of being pushed away by an irritated, morose Sam, but above all needing to share his hurt. She locked the front door of the house. Sam usually did that when he came in. She didn't bother to close the door that led to her rooms, or to turn out the lights downstairs. It wouldn't hurt them to burn through the night.

If he heard her coming up the stairs, he showed no sign of it as she entered his room. She closed the door to his room behind her, and locked it. He would not

want Neil to see him like this. He was sitting on the edge
of his bed, an unopened bottle of whisky in his hands.
He must have taken it from the cabinet in the living-
room.

She reached back and turned off the light-switch, then
moved to him and took the bottle from his hands. She
set it down on the floor. His hands were very cold. It
frightened her that he did not respond when she touched
his face, that he did not resist as she took off his jacket
and started to undo the buttons of his shirt.

Damn! His skin was so cold, even the flesh of his
shoulders and chest. Would it be better for him to have
some of the whisky? 'Sam, help me. You've got to get
under the covers, get warm.' He hadn't done up his cuffs,
so she was able to pull the shirt off, although she had
to yank to free the shirt-tail tucked into the back of his
trousers.

No tie. Cuffs unbuttoned. 'You were operating?' She
knelt down in front of him and undid his shoes. If only
he would answer! If only she could get him talking! He
was sitting on the edge of the bed, now undressed except
for his trousers, but he didn't even seem to know she
was there.

She pulled the covers back and pushed him down, then
she tried to figure out how she was going to get his
trousers off. He was much bigger than her, heavier, and
he wasn't co-operating.

'Leave me alone,' he said, his eyes staring up and
seeming to see her at last. She shook her head and pulled
the leather of his belt free of the loop.

'Alex!' His voice was hoarse. 'For goodness' sake!
Get out of here!'

She swallowed and watched the brass buckle coming
free of the leather. She pulled and the belt slipped out
from under him. She dropped it to the floor. She wasn't

sure if she could tackle his trousers but at least, without the belt, he would be a little more comfortable.

'I need to be alone, Alex.' He was lying near the edge of the bed, an arm thrown across his eyes. She undid the sash of her housecoat and let the robe fall to the floor. She had to climb over him before she could lie beside him. He said hoarsely, 'Please get out of here, honey.'

She touched his unruly dark hair, the dry flesh at his temple. He still felt cold. She drew the blankets up over them both, then she pulled his arm away from his face, drew it around her shoulders.

'Please let me stay, Sam,' she whispered, fitting her softness to his cool hardness. 'Don't send me away.' A shudder seemed to go through him. He turned slightly towards her, his arm tightening around her. She cupped his face with her hands and smoothed the tension gently with her thumbs.

'Sam, who did you operate on?' He jerked, but couldn't seem to pull himself away. In the moonlight shining through the window she could see his face, still pale and rigid. There was a faint sheen of moisture on the lashes of his closed eyes. Somehow, she had to get him to talk about it.

'Who was it?' she asked again.

'Celia.' His head rolled on the pillow. She kissed the closed eyes softly and felt him tremble. 'Celia Mallory.'

She wished that she could have recognised the name. It might have helped her to know the questions to ask. She remembered the call he had received hours earlier at the MacAvoys'. 'Was it a car accident?' He was shivering. She got her arms around him and burrowed her face into the coolness of his throat. 'Why did they call you?'

'My patient, and the OB-GYN man is out of town.'
His arms gripped her, hard, and she drew her leg up so
that they could be close all along their lengths, so that
he could have whatever warmth was hers. She felt a
massive shudder go through him and didn't know what
to do except to hold on more tightly. The silence grew
too long, but she could feel that he was not resting, that
the tension was still all through him.

'Sam, what happened?'

He buried his face into the fine softness of her hair.
'They were out for a drive. He—her husband had been
out of town, looking for work. He'd just got back and
they were celebrating.' Sam swallowed, said hoarsely, 'I
didn't know that till later, talking to him after—— He
had found a good job, and they had a baby coming in
a few weeks. They got a baby-sitter for their two kids
and went out. They were driving out to the picnic site
at Telegraph Point.' He shuddered. 'That was where he
had proposed to her. Five years ago.'

The woman had died, perhaps on the operating table.
Alex didn't know the details, and she wasn't sure if Sam
was going to be able to tell her, but she knew that he
had done everything he could to save Celia. He was
holding her very tightly, but she managed to free herself
enough to press soft lips against his cheek.

'It was no good from the beginning.' His lips found
hers and she drew his kiss into her, trying to give him
whatever she could of herself, hoping something would
help. He whispered against her mouth, 'We couldn't stop
the bleeding. Oh, lord, Alex! I tried everything,
but——'

She kissed the tears away from his cheeks, ran her
fingers through his hair and pressed her lips against his
eyes. He said dully, 'Alan thought there was a chance
for the baby. I delivered it—C-section. It was a boy. If

anyone could have saved it, I think Alan would have.'
His hands sought the softness of her curves. She didn't
think he realised that the tears were flowing down his
cheeks. 'Alex, I—I keep trying to think, to—— If there
was anything else I might have done. If—— She was so
damned happy the last time I saw her!'

She rubbed the hard rigidity of his back, smoothed
the harsh lines of his face with her lips. Slowly, she felt
the tension leaving him, felt him stroking her through
the nightgown as if touching could heal. Then his hands
stilled on her. She could hear his breathing deepen and
he slept, holding her closely against him. A car drove
past outside and light swept around the room, reflected
and twisted by the glass of the window. She saw his face
as the light moved across it, smooth except for the one
scar high on his cheekbone. Very vulnerable.

She slept then, lightly, aware of his touch, half waking
each time he shifted. As the sky lightened, waiting for
the sun to rise, she felt him move away from her, heard
a breath that was almost a groan. She opened her eyes.
He was leaning on his side, propped on one elbow,
staring down at her. There was no smile on his lips. His
eyes were very dark and deep. She stared up at him,
losing herself in his eyes, seeing things she had not seen
since that night they met.

The blanket was tumbled around her waist, the thin
white nightgown twisted around her, pulled tight under
her breasts. His eyes left hers, following the lines that
curved to her breasts, her hips, the round swelling that
was their child growing inside her.

His hand touched her shoulder, fingers drifting down
to brush the soft roundness of her breasts. She felt her
nipples growing rigid as he touched her, saw his quickly
indrawn breath as he stared down at her. Then his palm
brushed over the turgid peak of her breast and she

gasped, feeling the heat surging everywhere, all through her. She felt her lips parting, her eyes closing, hands seeking the curling hairs on his upper chest.

He stroked the tingling, swollen nipple, then drew his hand slowly, lightly, along the curve of her abdomen. She shivered, eyes opening to stare up at him. His lashes concealed his feelings and she wished sharply that she had the slender curves he had made love to four months ago.

'Alex,' he whispered, his lips bending to touch hers, moving to caress her breast through the nightgown. 'I want to see you.' His voice was hoarse and muffled. 'Please...'

She trembled as he pushed the thin nightgown up. He lifted her slightly, drew the wispy fabric over her head and threw it away, not bothering to look where it fell. Her fingers found the curling hairs of his chest and clenched, making him gasp as he stared down at her. She closed her eyes, embarrassed as she had not been when he made love to her under the trees.

'Oh, lord, darling! You're so——' his hand trembled, touching the roundness of her breast '—so incredibly beautiful.'

He was very gentle, his lips and his hands seeming to know how incredibly sensitive her flesh had grown with her pregnancy. He touched and kissed, making her tremble against the rigid need she could feel in him.

She groaned aloud when he took the peak of her breast into his mouth, his tongue moving gently, driving her insane with a stroking that stirred her right through to the centre of her womanhood. She laced her fingers through his hair, feeling the strength and passion of him, pulling his head up and opening her lips to his, giving him everything in her kiss, feeling her breasts squeezed hard against the muscles of his chest, his hair rough against her softness, his leg hard against her thigh as his hand moved down to her hips, pulling her close to feel his need.

She thought she would die of needing him, wanting him. 'Please,' she whispered, her hands slipping down over his shoulders, his back, touching the rigidity of his abdomen. 'Please love me,' she begged, unable to keep the words back.

He silenced her with his mouth on hers, then she lost track of the room, the rising sun, the world. There was only Sam's hands, Sam's lips, Sam's touch taking her beyond the edge of the world. She knew only the rough gentleness of his fingers as they brought fire to her skin, the soft moistness that was his mouth, the hardness that was his man's need.

When she was crying out his name, spinning beyond help, he drew her up over him and she felt his hands on her hips, the hard ridges of the muscles of his thighs. Then he thrust deep into her and she was clutching his shoulders, kneading his chest with heated hands, swept with him in a rising crescendo that climaxed, shaking them both to their foundations, leaving them trembling in each other's arms in a spinning aftermath that slowly transformed itself into warmth and closeness and security and . . . sleep.

CHAPTER TEN

'HERE,' said Dr Box, tearing the paper from his prescription pad. 'I want you to pick this up at the chemist. Sam felt you should have an additional iron supplement, and I'm inclined to agree. Your blood count's not drastically low, but——'

'Sam?' She stared down at the paper with its half-legible writing, feeling her pulse pounding just from the sound of his name.

'Sam,' he agreed, grinning at her across the desk. He had examined her, and everything was fine except for the mildly low iron count. 'I hope you're planning to be a good patient, because I can tell you that it's hell having a doctor as an expectant father. He's going to be dogging my footsteps until this baby's born.'

Sam had promised her that no one was going to be in any doubt as to who was the father of this child. Certainly her doctor had no doubt. She smiled a little and he said sourly, 'You'd better marry him. It might improve his temper.'

'We'll see,' she said, her fingers trembling as she put the paper away.

'Four weeks,' he called after her as she left. 'And be sure you get in here on time. And take those pills.'

'I will,' she promised.

She didn't see Sam, but she heard his voice through the door to one of the examining-rooms. Yesterday she had fully intended to come to this appointment and ask Dr Box for the name of a good doctor in the Victoria

area, near Aunt Lexie's empty house. She had hoped
that she could get in and out of here without seeing Sam.
Now she felt a sharp pain of disappointment that he was
behind that door, that she would have to go away and
wonder whether he would come home early tonight.

He had not called her on the telephone this morning.
She had waited, hoping he would call, but the phone
had been silent all morning except for a brief call from
her agent.

'The publisher wants to know when you'll be
submitting that next book. How about it? How's it
going?'

She had closed her eyes and tried to think about the
book, the chapters that had been unfolding so quickly
a few days ago. 'Two months,' she promised tentatively,
telling herself that she would get back to work soon.
Tomorrow. Or next week. As soon as she could think
murder again.

There would be no ferry, despite the fact that she had
woken this morning alone in Sam's bed. He must have
left very quietly, careful not to wake her. She had wanted
to be up with him, making the breakfast that he always
skipped.

She knew that his slipping away before she woke was
not a good sign. He had not kissed her to wake her. She
knew why. He had woken remembering the night before,
remembering that she had seen his pain and sorrow over
losing Celia Mallory and her baby.

She had been blind until last night, thinking of herself
and her own problems, afraid of what other people might
think because she was the pastor's daughter and she was
having a baby. It had taken last night to open her eyes,
seeing how afraid he had been of letting her see his hurt
and his need. He was terrified of rejection, of letting

himself be seen to have emotional dependencies. He was
always giving to other people, but afraid to ask anything
for himself. She had been so busy feeling sorry for
herself, seeing Sam as strong and invulnerable. She had
been blind to his real needs. Maybe he would never be
able to say the words to her, but he loved her, and he
needed her.

Today he might push her away in a defensive reaction.
She was almost positive that he was avoiding seeing her
now, at the clinic. Or was she being paranoid? Dr Box
had talked as if Sam knew she was coming today, but
maybe...

She swallowed, walking quickly down the corridor to
the waiting-room. It didn't matter. Even if he pushed
her away, avoided her, she was not going to go away.
Not now. She would be waiting for him when he came
home. If he was uncomfortable around her, she would
somehow put him at ease. Dinner, she decided. She
would buy something nice for dinner, and ask him to
have a game of chess with her afterwards. He enjoyed
relaxing in the living-room after dinner, listening to the
stereo and talking in low, easy voices.

Neil had told her over breakfast that he was going out
to dinner with a college friend, then taking in a movie.
That meant she would be alone with Sam. She would
be careful, casual, as if last night had not happened.
After a while he would relax.

Maybe he would reach across the chess table and touch
her hair as he sometimes had. If he touched her, moved
to kiss her, she would let him know without words that
she was available for him. Maybe——

No! She must not expect anything. If she let the wants
loose she might be begging him for everything, anything
he could give. She wanted to be in his bed every night,

making his breakfasts in the mornings. She wanted to be what he came home to, his love. She wanted to hold his child in her arms and see him watching as if the woman and the child were everything he would ever want.

'Mary!' It was Mrs Bramley, waving a piece of paper, her greying hair wild around her cap, calling Alex back as she started to pull the door open. 'Here! Dr Dempsey left this for you!'

Everyone in the waiting-room seemed to be staring at her as she walked back towards the receptionist. Someone came through the front door and a gust of wind came in, pressing her loose jacket against her, emphasising the curve of her pregnancy.

Well, let them see. They probably all knew in any case. It would be common knowledge that Mary Houseman was losing her figure, and there would be no trouble guessing why. It was going to be a beautiful baby. Her baby, and Sam's. She hoped it was a boy with dark unruly hair. She smiled a little as she took the envelope from Mrs Bramley's fingers and the woman smiled back, saying obscurely, 'Dr Dempsey said to tell you his car's out back in the parking lot.'

She couldn't open it there with everyone watching. She made her way out, and avoided tripping over the toddler who was dragging a toy bus across the floor. Outside, the sun was almost painfuly brilliant. She wanted to tear open the envelope, but she was afraid.

Coward. She would go to the restaurant across the street and have a cup of coffee, sit down and take a deep breath. Then she would open it. She went four or five steps, then her fingers tore the envelope open, feeling a bulge through the paper. He had written Alex Houseman on the front of the envelope. Inside, on a prescription form, the dark ink said simply, 'Have dinner with me tonight? Please. I'll pick you up at six. Use my car and I'll take your scooter home.'

His car keys were there. Last month he had insisted that she stop riding her bicycle, and she knew that he did not like her riding the scooter either.

'It's dangerous,' he had asserted one night when she had been stubbornly resistant to his insistence that she stop riding it at least until the baby came, and let him get her a car to take its place. 'If you ever got hit by a car——'

'I'm careful,' she had countered and he had finally dropped the argument, but she knew that it bothered him.

She closed her hands around the keys. In a way she had been shutting him out, too, by refusing almost everything he offered. She had felt that she could only accept things for the child, that she must maintain her independence. She had been determined that she would take nothing more than she had to—unless he offered love. Selfish woman, she thought, staring down at the paper, seeing his name printed on the top of the form and his words written to her. 'Please,' he had said. Love was the word she had been holding out for, but it was not there. She remembered his eyes, his arms around her. He loved her. She had to believe that because it had been in his eyes and it was in all his actions.

She went back into the waiting-room, threaded her way past all the people. She recognised one or two of the women and she smiled at them. They smiled back and one said, 'Hello, Mary.' She would be the first one on her telephone when she got home tonight, probably telling Emily Derringer all about it.

Amazingly, Alex found that she did not care.

She put the keys to her scooter on the desk in front
of Mrs Bramley and said, 'Would you give those to Dr
Dempsey. He's not going to be able to get my scooter
started without them.' The woman looked up, startled,
and Alex added, 'And tell him I'll be waiting for him
at six.'

She felt her heart pounding as she went out, and she
knew they were all staring at her, but she felt good, as
if she had done something wonderful.

She eased his car out of the car park very carefully.
She had never driven it before. It was smooth and
powerful and very responsive. She drove it three blocks
to the chemist and prayed that no one would come
screaming through a stop sign and hit her. It would be
terrible if she bashed up Sam's car. She was positive that
he had never before let anyone else drive it.

If he offered to buy her a car again, she thought she
had better accept. She supposed he could afford it, and
it was impossible for her to drive this beautiful white
beast every day. She grinned at the thought of Dr
Dempsey tearing around town on her scooter. Definitely
not the image of a professional doctor, yet he had said
that he liked to dress the part when he was working.

She found herself giggling as she locked up the car,
imagining him in leather motorcycle jacket, jeans and
leather boots. It was easy to imagine, and he would look
great dressed like a biker—sexy and...not very medical.

She laughed aloud and felt love for him sweeping over
her. Sam, she thought as she dropped his keys, scram-
bling in a puddle of water to retrieve them. The keys
were just on a plain ring and she thought that she might
buy him a key-ring if she could find something nice in
the chemist.

She almost careered straight into Emily Derringer's back as she came through the doors into the chemist. Automatically, she ducked quickly around the end of the first aisle, out of sight of Emily, her heart pounding with panic.

Then she stopped, staring blankly at the rack of chocolate bars in front of her. Emily. How many times in the last few weeks had she seen that immaculate head of hair and turned away before she was seen herself? She couldn't run away from one gossipy woman all her life. She took a deep breath and tried to feel calm and courageous, tried to tell herself it wasn't going to matter when Emily turned that cold, critical gaze on her.

All right. She would make it quick.

She picked up a chocolate bar from the rack in front of her. Something to buy, a reason for being here. With a faint tinge of hysteria she realised that this was the same chemist where she had run into Emily while buying the pregnancy test kit.

She paid for the chocolate and accepted it back, bagged and stapled. Now she was ready for a quick exit. Emily was in the next aisle. Alex moved quickly towards her.

'Mary!'

'Hello, Mrs Derringer.' She pushed her hair back, said hurriedly, 'Nice to see you.'

She was going to move away, quickly, but amazingly the woman was smiling, saying, 'I've been hoping to run into you. How are you?'

'I—fine.' There was nothing in her eyes but warmth and that was impossible.

Emily was several inches taller than Alex. She frowned a little, looking down and saying, 'Come and have a cup

of tea with me. There's a restaurant next door and
I——'

'Oh, no, thank you.' Alex shook her head, edged away.
'I'd better go. I——'

'Please, Mary!' Emily had a paperback book in her
hands. She pushed it back into the rack beside her and
said urgently, 'I really do want to talk to you! I've been
hoping I'd run into you.'

No one could withstand a determined Emily Derringer.
Alex gave up trying, and found herself swept out of the
chemist and into a booth in the small restaurant next
door. It couldn't last forever. She would listen, harden
herself and somehow look as if she didn't care. Then it
would be over, and she would escape, go home and wait
for Sam.

'Now,' said Emily with determination as the waitress
left them with a steeping pot of tea and two empty cups
waiting. 'Tell me. Are you certain that you are all right?'

'I'm fine.' Alex licked her lips, avoided Emily's intent
gaze. This was not what she had expected, and she did
not know what to make of it.

'I want you to know——' Emily's voice broke off.

'You want me to know——' repeated Alex mechanically. 'What?'

'I——' Emily pushed at her hair. Alex watched the
rigid order of Emily's hairstyle being knocked out of
shape. 'I admire you very much,' said Emily finally,
abruptly.

Alex shook her head, not understanding. Surely Emily
knew. 'I'm going to have a baby, Mrs Derringer. I'm
pregnant.'

'I know.' Emily picked up the teapot and poured the
amber liquid into both cups, her hand trembling. 'That's
what I'm talking about.' She put the pot down, picked

up a jug and added cream, stirring carefully. Amazingly, the woman was nervous. 'I didn't have the—the guts you had.' Emily's hand kept stirring as she said, 'When I—— It happened to me, Mary, but I didn't have the courage to—— My parents were well off and they arranged everything. I just let them. They sent me to a doctor they knew, down in Seattle. I—I've always wished I'd had the courage to say no, to keep that baby.'

What had Sam said? Something about even Emily Derringer being human. 'Mrs Derringer——'

'Emily,' said the woman. 'I wish you would call me Emily.' She finally set the spoon down and met Alex's eyes. 'I hear you're calling yourself Alex these days?' She sounded a bit like the woman Alex was used to, her voice slightly acid.

Alex grinned. 'It's bit more appropriate than Mary, don't you think?' She glanced down at the waistline that had been disappearing over the last weeks and they laughed together.

'Mary—Alex, if there's anything I can do——' Alex shook her head and Emily said, 'If you need a loan—I know Dr Dempsey is a very good man, and he's been taking you under his wing. He's done a lot for the MacKenzie boy, too, and I was glad to see that. That boy badly needs a good man to look up to. I've been glad you had someone, too, but you want to have choices. If you need——'

Alex found herself saying, 'Sam's the baby's father,' a little surprised to realise that Emily had not known that. So much for Emily knowing everything. 'I love him,' she added. Maybe Emily would tell everyone in town what she was hearing now, but somehow Alex didn't think she would.

I'll tell him myself, she decided suddenly. Even if he can't say it, I will. Sam, I love you.

'I'd like you both to come to dinner one evening,' said Emily. 'You name the date. We'll get one of Harry's salmon out of the freezer and roast it.' The Derringers always had good salmon. Harry was a fisherman and he liked to save a few of the choicest Sockeye for his own family. She wondered how Sam would like Harry Derringer.

Then she was amazed to find herself confiding, 'Emily, I've got a problem. No, not the baby. That secret is out. I guess everyone in town knows about it, but—well, I don't quite know how to tell people about my other secret.'

Emily's eyes were lit with curiosity and Alex found herself grinning, enjoying being able to give this woman the first chance at something that might just surprise the parish more than the fact that Mary Houseman was pregnant and living with the new doctor.

'It's *Holy Murder*.'

'Murder?' Emily was bewildered.

Alex laughed. 'Yes, killing, but no, I'm not a murderer. I wrote a book. A murder mystery. The first victim gets murdered in a church pew in the middle of the night.'

Emily was nodding, not even looking surprised. 'You always did have a lively imagination. I remember Mr Woller up at the high school saying you were very creative behind that quiet smile. If you've written a book, I'd like to read it. I like mysteries. Have you sent it anywhere yet? They say you've got to be persistent, keep sending it out and don't give up no matter how many rejections you get.'

She enjoyed giving the news that *Holy Murder* was going to press in February. Before the pot of tea was gone, she found Emily deep in a plan to approach the bookshop and make sure there were plenty of copies ordered.

'I wouldn't have the nerve,' said Alex nervously.

'I would,' said Emily. 'I'd better read the book, if you don't mind, so I can tell him how good it is, but of course you've got to have a signing party there when it's published.' Emily was eagerly planning her new project. Two projects. Championing Alex's two babies—the human one, and the one that was going to press.

Sam's car was warm inside from the sun. Alex sat in it for a moment before starting the engine, then she decided to make one more stop before she went home. She was going to buy a dress, something special for tonight.

She hesitated on the threshold of the maternity-wear store, then went in. She had been putting this off, trying to stretch her clothes around a growing baby. The owner of the store was warm and enthusiastic, helping her to find something very special. The warm rust colours of the dress they chose together brought out unexpected gold highlights in her brown hair. The soft folds of the rich fabric draped to emphasise the new fullness of her breasts in a way that she was breathlessly certain would be very hard for Sam to resist. Last night, there had been no doubt that Sam was very turned on by her pregnancy, by the fullness of her breasts and the hard curve of her belly.

She would be back for more clothes the next day, but for today she just wanted the one, special dress. The store was very expensive, but she wanted to look her best for him. She bought new lingerie, too, and it was breathtakingly expensive for a few scraps of black lace. She wrote out the cheque and deliberately did not add up the new balance in her bank account.

She had just enough time to go home and wash her hair before he came home, giving it a cream rinse to bring out even more of the highlights. First, though, she had better go back to the chemist and get the pills Dr Box had told her to take. She grinned, feeling smugly happy in the knowledge that Sam would be sure to ask about the pills; and at the same time nervously apprehensive about seeing him after the intimacy of last night.

CHAPTER ELEVEN

WHEN Mrs Bramley brought Alex's scooter key to him, Sam decided nervously that maybe it was going to be all right. He had left Alex that morning, afraid to wake her and see regret in her eyes, but as soon as he had got to the hospital for his morning rounds he had started to worry.

What if she woke and took his absence to mean— what? That he regretted making love to her? He remembered her arms around him, her lips soft on his face, her voice low and careful as she tried to get him to talk about what had happened up at the hospital. As if his pain was more important to her then her own fears. She must love him. How else could she have responded to him as she had last night?

A sceptical voice in the back of his mind scoffed, insisting that it was only sex, physical attration, hormones and healthy bodies. He had to remember who his love was. A minister's daughter. She had been brought up with other people's need. Of course she had wanted to reach out and comfort him. That was all it had been.

But her eyes, dark and molten with everything she was giving him. He could not forget her eyes. And——

No one had ever seen him cry before. He could not quite understand why that did not bother him more. There were few enough times that he had let himself lose control like that, and never with anyone else watching. She had always seemed able to do that to him, to slip through the barriers into the vulnerable child that he hid from the world.

All day he swung from one emotional extreme to the other. The instinct to withdraw from the vulnerable intimacy of last night was always sharply overwhelmed by his terror that she might leave. Last night at dinner he had watched her, knowing that she was planning to leave him. What had changed now? Only him. He was even more dependent on this woman after last night, needed her even more desperately, yet was frightened of seeing rejection in her eyes.

He had seen the time of her appointment in the book, and he had left the note with the receptionist, unable to face her here in front of other people. His pen had hovered as he wrote, almost writing the words 'I love you' before he signed his name. In the end, he had simply signed his name, then had spent the next hour not knowing if that was right.

He hoped she would not be angry about his asking her to take his car. After last night, after Celia Mallory's tragedy, he had had living nightmares every time he thought of Alex out in traffic on a flimsy scooter. He was almost convinced that she would not accept the offer of his car, afraid she would not. After all, what had she let him give her? The apartment, and only that with a fight, a ridiculous insistence that she pay.

Roy came into his office shortly after four-thirty. 'You OK?' he asked gruffly.

Sam pushed his hands through his hair and tried to feel calm and rational. It had been going around and around in his head all afternoon. She had taken his car. He'd looked out and saw it gone, and he had her scooter keys in his pocket. She would be there, waiting for him.

But what was he going to say to her?

Lord! He had never been so frightened in his life before! 'No,' he told Roy abruptly, somehow unable to lie. 'I'm not OK.' He closed his eyes. The old Sam had never confided feelings or uncertainties in anyone, but ever since the day he had met Alex his life had been turning around, upside down, and he knew he would never be the same man again.

'Can I do anything?' asked Roy.

Sam shook his head. 'I'm going to ask her to marry me again.' He closed his eyes briefly and said, 'At least, I think that's what I'm going to say to her.'

Roy shook his head and said, 'Sam, why don't you tell her that you love her. You've never told her that, have you? Do it and let the rest of it look after itself.'

Sam tried to imagine himself saying those words and he couldn't do it. 'I'm scared,' he admitted. He tried to laugh but it didn't come off.

'You're stupid if you don't,' said Roy sharply. He put his hand on the door and said, 'Get out of here. Go home and settle this.'

'I've got patients to see,' he said automatically, reaching for the chart on his desk. He realised that he was afraid to go, that six o'clock was going to come too soon and he would not be ready.

'Mrs Olsen and her son cancelled,' said Roy briskly. 'The rest, I can cover for you. Get the hell out of here, Sam! Slip out the back way and go home. You've done enough for one day.'

It took him almost half an hour to go a mile on Alex's scooter—five minutes of driving and almost twenty to extricate himself from the RCMP officer who pursued him with his siren going.

His car was there, parked where he always parked it. He rolled her scooter under the carport, taking his time about it, telling himself that he was not stalling. He was trying to practise words for her, but none of them were right. Please don't go. Let me look after you. I...need you, his mind finished, but he could feel the panic of even thinking like that.

What could he give her? How could he make her want to stay? What had a man like him to offer a warm, wonderful woman like Alex? Alex Diamond, fantasy lady, all heat and passion barely concealed under a smooth, reserved exterior.

He went in because he could not stay outside forever.

Inside his foyer he found the door to her rooms open and he went in, still trying frantically to form the right words, terribly afraid that there were no right words. She was not in her living-room. He heard the sound of water and went on into her bedroom, stopping in the open door to her bathroom. He felt his heart pounding at the sight of her. For a second he was afraid that he would start trembling wildly with his need for her.

She was dripping wet from the bath, little streams of water running down her breasts. She had a towel in one hand, reaching around to dry her back, stretching the white skin tight across the swelling of her fertility.

She became very still when she saw him. He thought that she would pull the towel around to conceal herself from him, but she didn't. She straightened, her lips parting slightly, her eyes staring at his. He was not sure what the message was in the deep brown of her gaze.

He wanted desperately to reach out and touch the beautiful womanliness of her, but he was afraid to seem too grasping. Last night she had given herself to him again, but he must not assume that she was his to take at a whim. He took a deep, ragged breath and felt the stiffness of his arousal.

'Alex,' he whispered, finding himself moving closer, knowing he was going to lose this battle, that he must touch her. He licked his dry lips.

Her voice was weak, just a whisper. 'Sam, I was going to——' She pushed back wet tendrils of hair. 'I bought a new dress. I was going to—wanted to look nice for you.'

'You're beautiful.' He took the towel and started to dry her, rubbing the full breasts through the terry. 'You're always beautiful.'

She licked her lips and he had to bend down, to taste her sweetness. 'Sam,' she whispered, and she was in his arms, warm and wet and wonderful. He held her carefully, just feeling the warmth of her and trying to store it up for memories in case this was the last time. He tried to remember the words he had planned, but none of them was right.

'Darling.' He felt her cheek under his lips and kissed gently, moving again to her mouth and feeling her arousal growing as he held her, as his tongue explored the warm darkness of her mouth.

She whispered, 'I was afraid this morning—I thought you wouldn't want to see me.'

'Oh, lord!' He groaned against her lips. He loved the feel of her, the tightness that was her growing womb, the swelling that was nature's preparation of her breasts for motherhood. He wished he could tell her how much he loved her, but he could not get the words out and he took refuge instead in the sweetness of her body, lifting her and carrying her to the bed, looking down at her and marvelling that her eyes were warm and inviting, that her arms curled up around his shoulders and urged him closer.

'We should close the doors,' she whispered as his lips came against hers.

He said raggedly, 'I don't know if I can walk straight,' and her laughter was warm against his mouth, somehow giving him the courage to say, 'And I'm afraid to let go of you. I'm terrified you'll leave me.'

She was very silent then, and he pulled away before he could see what was in her eyes. He closed the door that led into the foyer, and locked it. Then he came slowly back to the bedroom, remembering that other time when she had told him that she could not be his lover and still face the people of this town.

She saw the uncertainty in his eyes as he came back. She wanted to tell him that she loved him, that it was all right, but she wasn't sure if it was the right thing to say. Would it make him feel trapped? She didn't want to do that. He closed the bedroom door as he came in, locking it. Then he leaned against the closed door and stared at her, not coming closer.

'I'm not going to leave you,' she managed to say. She tried to read his eyes, to know if he wanted to hear this, but his face was harsh and shuttered. She got up off the bed, picking up the robe and belting it around her. It didn't fit as well as it had once, but she needed something to cover herself from his bleak gaze. He looked terrible, as if he were sick.

She moved closer to him, touched his arm fleetingly and drew her hand back. 'Sam, I'm not leaving unless you send me away.' He didn't say a word. She swallowed. 'Sam, are you going to send me away?'

'No.' His voice was ragged. He gulped and said, 'I think we should get married.'

She bit her lip. Why was he saying that? She wished she could read what was in his eyes. If only she hadn't sent him to close the doors. He had been close to her, touching her, his eyes telling her that he needed her. Now...

'Why?' She touched him, her fingers resting on his chest. She wanted to come closer, to flow up against him and make him need her again, as he had a moment ago. What was it? Was he regretting what he'd said? 'Why do you think we should get married, Sam?'

He shook his head. She wished he didn't look so pale. Oh, lord! What was she doing? He was the man who couldn't reach out, could not ask, who could only give; and here she was demanding reasons from him, asking for declarations when he could not give them.

'It's all right,' she said quickly, her fingers pressing against his chest, feeling a heavy heartbeat. 'I——'

'I've been having nightmares about you leaving me,' he said raggedly. 'I——'

'Sam, you don't need to say anything.' She stepped closer and put her arms around him, felt his tension. 'I'll——'

His lips smothered her words, his arms coming around her. 'Darling, I'm having a very hard time with this.' She pressed her lips against his and he kissed her, hard. 'I'm afraid I'm not very good at this. I——'

'It doesn't matter,' she insisted, her fingers flowing through his hair. It really didn't matter if he said the words. She could see it in his eyes, feel it in his arms trembling as they held her. 'I love you, Sam.'

She saw his eyes flash, felt the tension draining out of him. 'Are you sure? You——'

'I'm sure.' She touched his hair, drew gentle fingers along the harsh contours of his face. 'I've always known,' she whispered. 'The first time I saw you, I knew—it just took me a while to come to terms with it. I had some growing up to do.'

He laughed, holding her close, his eyes seeming to light from inside. 'You? What about me?' He swung her up into his arms and carried her over to the bed and said in a low growl, 'I don't want you to think that I just want you for your body, but I've been dreaming about you all day—oh, darling! I've been dreaming about you from the first moment I saw you. I've—my life had turned upside down, as if——' He leaned over her, his eyes dark, his hands touching her as if he knew that she was his, always and any time that he needed her. He said, slowly and with difficulty, 'Alex, I've never been in love before.'

She was very still. His eyes closed, then opened again, meeting hers. She swallowed and said, 'Sam, you don't have to say it.'

'I love you,' he said, very softly. 'I've loved you forever, I think, and I hope you're going to marry me, because I don't think I can settle for less.'

'Yes,' she whispered, but he didn't seem to hear.

He said slowly, 'I know it's upsetting you, wondering what people are saying about you and—— They'll accept it, Alex. Even if you don't want to marry me yet, they'll come around. If—once we're married no one will think anything of it, and—honey, if it bothers you, wondering if they're talking—just give me a little time and I'll work out something. We can move if you want, or——'

'I don't want to move.'

He didn't seem to hear her. 'So long as we're together. Alex, I swear I can make you happy! You—I can't—I couldn't face the thought of your leaving.' He sucked in a ragged breath, said, 'I'm greedy. I want it all. I want to wake up to the sound of our baby crying, to bring him to you and watch him sucking at your breast. I want—always, Alex. I want all the years, all of you.'

He was trembling. She took his face in her hands. 'Sam, I'm not leaving. I love you. You'd have to throw me out to get rid of me, and even then I don't think I would be willing to go without a fight. I—I'm going to marry you.'

She felt him shudder, then he took a deep breath and simply said, 'Good.' He touched her hair and said in a voice that tried to be casual, 'I think we should dry your hair before I make love to you.' She shivered at what was in his eyes, his voice, as he said, 'You must not catch cold. And I'm glad you're going to marry me, because the police are expecting an invitation to the wedding.'

'What?' She pushed herself up on to her elbows, staring at him. He smiled and shook his head, disappearing into the bathroom and returning a second later with a dry towel and a brush.

'Sit up and we'll get your hair dry,' he commanded.

She knew that he was still uncomfortable with his declaration of love. The words had been hard for him and she realised that he had to draw back a little even though he loved her deeply. She smiled and asked, 'What's this about the police?' She found herself sitting to his command, with Sam cross-legged on the bed behind her, rubbing her hair dry with the towel.

He did not answer her for a moment, but pushed the gown off her shoulder and pressed a kiss on to her neck. His voice was low and amused. 'I told the officer who stopped me that I wasn't responsible for my behaviour.

I was trying to get up my nerve to propose to the woman I loved.'

She trembled and knew that he felt it. 'You were speeding?' she accused.

'Not me,' he defended himself. 'I haven't run a red light in months, and I've been driving the Corvette as if it was a—an old maid's car.'

'That's not true!' She twisted around, found herself breathlessly facing him with only a few molecules of air between their lips. 'You were going sixty in a fifty zone on the way to the waterfront last night, and you know it! You—why did the police stop you?'

'I'm not sure.' He shrugged, grinning, looking like the kind of man a minister's daughter should be warned against. 'I think he just thought I looked suspicious. He was determined to find something, and he managed.'

'What?'

'No motorcycle endorsement on my licence.' His mouth was serious, but she saw the laughter in his eyes and knew he was going to tease her. 'I thought of fighting it,' he said slowly. 'I thought I could think up some grounds for defence, like being insane with love for the minister's daughter, not being in my right mind.'

'You got a summons?' She couldn't help the laughter, knowing that this was going to be all around town by the time the day was over. She murmured, 'You're going to be the disgrace of the town. Dr Dempsey getting a summons for driving Mary Houseman's motor scooter without a licence.'

'We need something for Emily to talk about.' He was smiling, then the smile faded and he said, 'Alex, don't worry. It'll be all right. When we're married, even your mother will come round.'

'It doesn't matter,' she said, and it was true. She reached for the man she loved, knowing that he loved her, knowing that everything else would look after itself so long as they were together.

Later, she would tell him that they were going to Emily's for dinner next week.

PENNY JORDAN

Sins and infidelities...
Dreams and obsessions...
Shattering secrets
unfold in...

THE HIDDEN YEARS

SAGE — stunning, sensual and vibrant, she spent a lifetime distancing herself from a past too painful to confront... the mother who seemed to hold her at bay, the father who resented her and the heartache of unfulfilled love. To the world, Sage was independent and invulnerable— but it was a mask she cultivated to hide a desperation she herself couldn't quite understand... until an unforeseen turn of events drew her into the discovery of the hidden years, finally allowing Sage to open her heart to a passion denied for so long.

The Hidden Years—a compelling novel of truth and passion that will unlock the heart and soul of every woman.

AVAILABLE IN OCTOBER!
Watch for your opportunity to complete your Penny Jordan set.
POWER PLAY and SILVER will also be available in October.

HIDDEN

Harlequin Superromance®

Available in Superromance this month
#462—STARLIT PROMISE

STARLIT PROMISE is a deeply moving story of a
woman coming to terms with her grief and gradually
opening her heart to life and love.

Author Petra Holland sets the scene beautifully, never
allowing her heroine to become mired in self-pity. It
is a story that will touch your heart and leave you
celebrating the strength of the human spirit.

**Available wherever Harlequin books
are sold.**

STARLIT-A

HARLEQUIN
Romance®

**This September, travel to England
with Harlequin Romance
FIRST CLASS title #3149,
ROSES HAVE THORNS
by Betty Neels**

It was Radolf Nauta's fault that Sarah lost her job at the hospital and was forced to look elsewhere for a living. So she wasn't
particulary pleased to meet him again in a totally different envi-
ronment. Not that he seemed disposed to be gracious to her:
arrogant, opinionated and entirely too sure of himself, Radolf
was just the sort of man Sarah disliked most. And yet, the
more she saw of him, the more she found herself wondering
what he really thought about her—which was stupid, because
he was the last man on earth she could ever love....

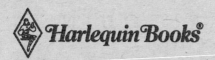

GREAT NEWS...
HARLEQUIN UNVEILS NEW SHIPPING PLANS

For the convenience of customers, Harlequin has announced that Harlequin romances will now be available in stores at these convenient times each month*:

Harlequin Presents, American Romance, Historical, Intrigue:

> May titles: April 10
> June titles: May 8
> July titles: June 5
> August titles: July 10

Harlequin Romance, Superromance, Temptation, Regency Romance:

> May titles: April 24
> June titles: May 22
> July titles: June 19
> August titles: July 24

We hope this new schedule is convenient for you.

With only two trips each month to your local bookseller, you'll never miss any of your favorite authors!

*Please note: There may be slight variations in on-sale dates in your area due to differences in shipping and handling.

*Applicable to U.S. only.

HDATES-RR

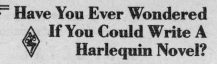

Have You Ever Wondered If You Could Write A Harlequin Novel?

Here's great news—Harlequin is offering a series of cassette tapes to help you do just that. Written by Harlequin editors, these tapes give practical advice on how to make your characters—and your story—come alive. There's a tape for each contemporary romance series Harlequin publishes.

Mail order only

All sales final

- ✂ -

Clip this coupon and return to:

HARLEQUIN READER SERVICE
Audiocassette Tape Offer
3010 Walden Ave.
P.O. Box 1396
Buffalo, NY 14269-1396

I enclose my check/money order payable to HARLEQUIN READER SERVICE for $5.70 ($4.95 + 75¢ for delivery) for EACH tape ordered. My total check is for $ _____ .
Please send me:

- ☐ Romance and Presents
- ☐ American Romance
- ☐ Superromance
- ☐ Intrigue
- ☐ Temptation
- ☐ All five tapes ($21.95 total)

Name: _____

Address: _____ Apt: _____

City: _____ State: _____ Zip: _____

NY residents add appropriate sales tax.

AUDIO-H1D